# THE DANCER
# FROM ATLANTIS

# THE
# DANCER
# FROM
# ATLANTIS

by POUL ANDERSON

NELSON DOUBLEDAY, INC.
Garden City, New York

# THE DANCER
# FROM ATLANTIS

AND THE seven angels which had the seven trumpets prepared themselves to sound.

And the first angel sounded, and there followed hail and fire mingled with blood, and they were cast upon the earth: and the third part of trees was burnt up, and all green grass was burnt up.

And the second angel sounded, and as it were a great mountain burning with fire was cast into the sea: and the third part of the sea became blood; and the third part of the creatures which were in the sea, and had life, died; and the third part of the ships were destroyed.

And the third angel sounded, and there fell a great star from heaven, burning as it were a lamp, and it fell upon the third part of the rivers, and upon the fountains of waters; and the name of the star is called Wormwood: and the third part of the waters became wormwood; and many men died of the waters, because they were made bitter.

And the fourth angel sounded, and the third part of the sun was smitten, and the third part of the moon, and the third part of the stars; so as the third part of them was darkened, and the day shone not for a third part of it, and the night likewise.

And I beheld, and heard an angel flying through the midst of heaven, saying with a loud voice, Woe, woe, woe, to the inhabiters of the earth by reason of the other voices of the trumpet of the three angels, which are yet to sound!

—Revelation, viii, 6–13

*Where is the fair   assemblage of heroes,*
*The sons of Rudra,   with their bright horses?*
*For of their birth   knoweth no man other,*
*Only themselves   their wondrous descent.*

*The light they flash   upon one another;*
*The eagles fought,   the winds were raging;*
*But this secret   knoweth the wise man,*
*Once that Prishni   her udder gave them.*

*Our race of heroes,   through the Maruts be it*
*Ever victorious   in reaping of men.*
*On their way they hasten,   in brightness the brightest,*
*Equal in beauty,   unequalled in might.*

—Rig-Veda, vii, 56
(*Max Müller, tr.*)

# ONE

"FULL MOON TONIGHT," he said. "Come up on deck with me. It should be beautiful."

"No, I'm tired," she answered. "You go. I'd rather stay here."

Duncan Reid made himself look squarely at his wife and say, "I thought this was *our* trip."

Pamela sighed. "Of course. Later, dear, please. I'm sorry to be such a rotten sailor, but I am. All the bad weather we've been having till now. Oh, the pills kept me from getting actually sick, but I never felt quite good either."

He continued to regard her. A dozen years ago, when they married, she was well endowed. Later a waxing plumpness became her despair, dieting her anguish. He had tried to say, "Don't weep over it. Take more exercise. Mainly, remember you're still a damned attractive woman." And she was, fair-complexioned, blue-eyed, with soft brown hair and regular features and gentle-looking mouth. But he was less and less often able to say it successfully.

"Seems I made a mistake, booking us onto a ship." He heard how bitterness tinged his voice, and saw that she did too.

"Well, you knew I can't go on your sailboat," she retorted. "Or backpacking or—" Her head drooped, as did her tone. "Let's not start that quarrel again."

His glance went past her, across the impersonal coziness of their cabin, to the picture of their children on the dresser. "Maybe we should," he replied slowly. "We don't have to worry about them for a while, what they might overhear. Maybe we should bring things out into the open at last."

"What things?" She sounded almost frightened. For an instant he saw her immaculate gown and grooming as armor. "What are you talking about?"

He retreated. "I . . . I can't find words. Nothing obvious. Spats over ridiculous issues, irritations we learned to live with very early in the game, or imagined we had—I'd, uh, I'd hoped this could be, well, I told you, a second honeymoon—" His tongue knotted up on him.

He wanted to cry something like: Have we simply been losing interest in each other? Then how? Nothing physical, surely; not to such a degree; why, I'm a mere forty, you thirty-nine, and we still have enough good times to know how many more we might have. But they've been getting steadily more rare. I've been busy and you, perhaps, have been bored in spite of your assorted bustling around; after dinner I'll read a book in my study while you watch television in the living room, till the first who grows sleepy says a polite goodnight and goes to bed.

Why won't you come on deck with me, Pam? What a night it must be for love! Not that I feel hot especially, but I want to feel hot, for you. I could, if you'd let me.

"I'm sorry," she repeated, and patted his hand. He wished he could tell how real the gesture was. "I am tired, though."

"Of me?" came out before he could stop it.

"No, no, no. Never." She came to him, laid arms around his waist. He patted her back. To him both motions felt automatic.

"We used to have adventures," he said. "Remember? Newly wed and poor and making do."

"I didn't think scrimping along in that horrible cramped apartment was an adventure." She broke off her words, but also from him. "Let me get my coat, darling."

"Not as a, uh, duty," he protested, knowing that was the wrong thing to say but not sure what would have been right.

"I've changed my mind. I could use a stroll." Her smile was extremely bright. "It's stuffy in here. And the ventilator's noisy."

"No, please. I understand. You do need rest." He stepped to the closet and fetched his own topcoat in one hurried motion. "And I'll be kind of galloping. Want to stretch my legs. You don't enjoy that." He avoided seeing her face as he departed.

Topside he did in fact stride himself breathless around and around the main deck. Once he went up to the forepeak, but left it after he came upon a young couple necking there. Presently he felt somewhat less churned and stopped by the rail for a smoke.

The wind, rain, fog, and heavy, hacking waves of springtime in the North Pacific had died down. The air was cool, alive with unnamed sea odors and a low breeze, and it was clear; despite the moon, he had seldom seen as many stars as glittered in that lucent blackness. The light lay in a shivering road across waters whose crests it made sparkle and whose troughs it made sheen like molten obsidian. They murmured, those waters, and rushed and hissed and lapped, most softly in their immensity, and took to themselves the throb of engines and gave back the slight trembling of hull and deck.

His pipe started, Reid cradled the bowl in his hand for a bit of warmth and hearthglow. He had always found peace on the sea. Lovely and inhuman. Lovely because inhuman? He'd attempted to make Pam see that, but she didn't care for Robinson Jeffers either.

He stared at the moon, low to aft. Does it make any difference to you that four men's footprints have marked you? he wondered. Recognizing the thought as childish, he looked outward and ahead. But yonder lay the seemingly endless war. And behind, at home, was the seemingly endless upward ratcheting of hate and fear; and Mark, and Tom (as he, a proud nine years of age, now insisted on being called), and little, little Bitsy, whom there was so short a time to cherish before they must walk forth into a world breaking apart beneath them. When you considered those things, what importance had two people, middle-class, slipping into middle age, other than what was conferred on them by the inverse square law?

Reid's mouth quirked wryly around the pipestem. He thought: Too bad you can't quantify the statics and dynamics of being human in neat vectors, or develop a tensor calculus for the stresses in a marriage. —The smoke rolled pungent over his tongue and palate.

"Good evening, sir."

Turning, Reid identified the moon-whitened shape: Mike Stockton, third engineer. Aboard a passenger-carrying freighter, acquaintanceships developed fast. However, he hadn't chanced to see much of this particular officer.

"Why, hello," he said reflexively. "Nice night, isn't it?"

"Sure is. Mind if I join you? I'm due on watch in a few minutes."

Am I lonely for everyone to see? wondered Reid. And then: Cut that out. You're at the point of sniveling. A bit of talk may well be precisely what you need. "Do stay. Think the weather will hold?"

"The forecasters do. The whole way to Yokohama, if we're lucky. Will you and your wife be in Japan long?"

"A couple of months. We'll fly back." The kids will be okay at Jack and Barbara's, Reid thought; but still, when we walk in that door and Bitsy sees her daddy and comes running on her stumpy legs, arms out and laughing—

"I know the country just enough to envy you." Stockton scanned Reid as if, in an amiable fashion, he meant it.

He saw a lanky, rawboned, wide-shouldered six-footer, a long craggy head, jutting nose and chin, heavy black brows over gray eyes, sandy hair, no-longer-fashionable turtleneck sweater beneath the coat. Even in the tuxedos he must sometimes wear, and after Pamela's most careful valeting, Reid managed to appear rumpled.

"Well, a business trip for me. I'm an architect, you may remember. Quit my job recently to form a partnership." Pamela didn't like the risk. But she'd liked less the drabness of semi-poverty in their first years, when he refused to accept a subsidy from her parents; and she'd stuck that out, and now they were in the 20-K bracket and if his try at independence failed (though he was bloody well resolved it wouldn't) he could always find another position somewhere. "Considering the strong Japanese influence in homebuilding nowadays," Reid went on, "I figured I'd sniff around after, well, all right, inspiration at the source. In provincial villages especially."

Pam might holler. She wanted her comfort. . . . No! He'd fallen into an ugly habit of doing her injustice. She'd joined his outings, and apologized afterward for spoiling them with a humbleness that came near breaking his heart, and finally stayed behind when he went. Had he tried as hard to interest himself in her bridge games, her volunteer work at the youth center and the hospital, even her favorite TV programs?

"You're from Seattle, aren't you, Mr. Reid?" Stockton asked. "I'm a native myself."

"I'm a mere immigrant, as of five years ago. Chicago previously, since getting out of the Army. Before then, Wisconsin, et cetera, back to dear old Boston. The American story."

Reid realized he was babbling of matters that could not imaginably interest the other man. It wasn't his usual behavior. If anything, he was too withdrawn unless a few beers or a couple of Scotches had relaxed him. Tonight he was seeking to escape his thoughts. And why not? If he'd shaken off the Presbyterian theology of his boyhood, did he have to carry around the associated conscience?

"Uh, I'd visited Seattle before and liked the place," he continued almost helplessly, "but at first the only halfway decent job offer I got was in Chicago. A concrete monstrosity, that town. They said there you'd better wear glasses, whether or not you needed them, or somebody would unscrew your eyeballs."

He'd kept remembering people who were relaxed and friendly, and boats white-winged on Puget Sound, and Mount Rainier's snowpeak floating high and pure above, and virgin forest a couple of hours' drive from downtown. To Pam, of course, Chicago was home. Well, Evanston was, which made a difference. When he finally landed a position in Seattle and they moved, she found the city a backwater, where the weather seemed to be mostly leaden skies, or rain, or fog, or rain, or snow, or rain. . . . Had he, waiting happily for the next cataract of sunshine, failed to notice how the rain gnawed at her?

"Yeah, we're lucky, I guess, living where we do," Stockton said. "Apart from those medieval liquor laws."

Reid chuckled. "Come, now. No medieval king would have dared pass liquor laws that barbaric."

Then, as his mood was lifting a trifle, Stockton told him, "I'd better go on to the engine room. Nice talking," and was quickly out of sight.

Reid sighed, leaned elbows on rail, and drew on his pipe. The night sea went *hush-hush-hush*. Tomorrow Pam might feel happier. He could hope for that, and hope Japan would turn out to be a fairytale as advertised, and beyond—

Beyond? His mind, free-associating, conjured up a globe. Besides excellent spatial perception, which he'd better have in his profession, he was gifted with an uncommon memory. He could draw the course if the ship continued past Yokohama. It wouldn't. The owners knew better. Reach Southeast Asia, or pretty close. Hard to understand that at this moment human beings were maiming and killing human beings whose names they would never know. Damn the ideologies! When would the torment be over? Or had every year always been tragic, would every year always be? Reid remembered another young man who died in another war, a lifetime ago, and certain lines he had written.

*The way of love was thus.*
*He was born one winter morn*
*With hands delicious,*
*And it was well with us.*

*Love came our quiet way,*
*Lit pride in us, and died in us,*
*All in a winter's day.*
*There is no more to say.*

Rupert Brooke could say it, though. Thanks for that, Dad. An English professor in a tiny Midwestern college hadn't had a lot of money for his children—wherefore Reid, earning his own, needed an extra year to graduate—but he gave them stubbornness about what was right, wide-ranging curiosity, the friendship of books—maybe too close a friendship, stealing time that was really Pam's. . . . No more brooding, Reid decided. A few final turns around the deck, and probably by then she'd have fallen asleep and he could do likewise.

He clamped the pipe between his teeth and straightened.

And the vortex seized him, the black thunders, he had no moment to cry in before he was snatched from the world.

# TWO

WHERE THE Dnieper snaked in its eastward bend, grassland gave way to high bluffs through which the river hastened, ringing aloud as it dashed itself over rocks and down rapids. Here ships must be unloaded and towed, in several places hauled ashore on rollers, and cargoes must be portaged. Formerly this had been the most dangerous part of the yearly voyage. Pecheneg tribesmen were wont to lurk nearby, ready to ride down upon the crews when these were afoot and vulnerable, plunder their goods and make slaves of whoever were not lucky enough to be killed. Oleg Vladimirovitch had been in one such fight as an apprentice. In it, by God's grace, the Russians sent the raiders off bewailing their own dead and took many husky prisoners to sell in Constantinople.

Things were far better since Grand Prince Yaroslav—what a man, cripple though he was!—trounced the heathen. He did it at the gates of Kiev, so thoroughly that ravens afterward gorged themselves till they could not fly and no Pecheneg was ever again seen in his realm. Oleg was in the host on that wondrous day: his first taste of real war, thirteen years ago, he a fuzzy-cheeked lout of seventeen winters. Later he rode against the Lithuanians, and later still sailed on the ill-fated expedition against the Imperial city. But mainly he was a trader, who wanted no troubles that cut into profit. (Tavern brawls didn't count, they nourished the soul, if you made sure to clear out before the Emperor's police arrived.) He was happy that the Greeks were likewise sensible and, soon after throwing back the Russians, resumed business with them.

"Yes," he said to the bumper of kvass in his hand, "peace and brotherly love, those are good for trade, as Our Lord preached when he walked this earth."

He stood on a clifftop overlooking the stream and the fleet. It was beneath the dignity of a shipowner to haul on cables or lug bales; and he had three vessels by now, not bad for a boy who in birchbark leggings had run traplines through northern woods. His skippers could oversee the work. But sentries were needed. Not that anyone expected bandits; however, the furs, hides, amber, tallow, beeswax being transported would fetch a price down south that just might draw many masterless land-loupers together for a single swoop.

"To you, Ekaterina Borisovna," Oleg said, raising his cup. It was for traveling, wooden, albeit silver-trimmed to show the world that he was a man of consequence at home in Novgorod.

While the thin sour beer went down, he was thinking less of his wife or, for that matter, various slave and servant girls, than of a tricksy little minx at journey's end last year. Would Zoe again be available? If so, that gave him an added reason, besides extending his connections among the foreign merchants resident in Constantinople, for wintering there. Though Zoe, hm, over several months Zoe might prove painfully expensive.

Bees hummed in clover, cornflowers blazed blue as the over-arching, sun-spilling sky. Below Oleg, men swarmed about the bright-hued, swan- and dragon-headed ships. They must be long-ing for the Black Sea: in oars and up mast, loaf and let the wind carry you on, never thinking about the currents, never caring that that was when the poor devil of an owner must worry most about a wreck. Their shouts and oaths were lost across a mile or two, blent into the clangor of great Father Dnieper. These heights knew quietness, heat, sweat trickling down ribs and soaking into the quilted padding beneath the chainmail coat, which began to drag on the shoulders, but high, high overhead a lark chanted, and the joy floated earthward while a mild buzz-ing from the beer rose to meet it. . . .

Oleg smiled at everything which lay in his tomorrows.

And the vortex took him.

Winters were less strong here than on the plains over which Uldin's forebears went drifting and storming. Here snowfall was scant, most years, and a man had no need to grease his face against the cold. But he could nevertheless lose livestock to hunger and weather if he did not ride the range and take care of his beasts—especially when lambing time drew near.

Uldin's followers numbered only half a dozen, including two unarmed slaves. The East Goths had fled into a Roman realm which would not likely prove hospitable. Some stayed, of course, the slain and those who were captured and beaten into meekness. For the past three years the Huns had lived in peace, settling into their newly conquered land.

It lay white beneath low gray clouds. Here and there stood leafless trees. The snags of a garth sacked and burnt were the last sign of farming. Fences had been torn down for firewood and grain had yielded to grass. Breath smoked on a raw wind. The hoofs of the ponies plopped in snow, clattered on ground frozen hard. Saddle leather squeaked and bits jingled.

Uldin's son Oktar edged alongside. He was barely old enough to ride along, his father being young, but already he showed in height and pale skin the Alanic blood of his mother. She had been Uldin's first woman, a slave given him by his own father when he reached an age to enjoy her. He finally lost her, gambling with a man of another tribe at a Sun Festival meeting, and didn't know what her life became afterward, though for a while he had idly wondered.

"We can reach camp tonight if we push hard," the boy said importantly. Uldin half raised his quirt and Oktar added in haste, "Honored sire."

"We won't," Uldin answered. "I'll not weary horses for you to sleep earlier in a warm yurt. We'll stretch our bags at—" he made a nomad's quick estimate—"Bone Place." Oktar's eyes widened and he gulped. Uldin barked a laugh. "What, afraid of wolf-scattered Gothic skeletons? If they alive couldn't stop us slaughtering them, who fears their thin ghosts? Say boo to

them." He jerked his head in dismissal and Oktar fell behind
with the rest.

Uldin would, in truth, also have liked to make the main en-
campment. Riding the range at this season was no sport. In
summer the entire tribe traveled with their herds, and a man
could nearly always be home at eventide after a day's work or
hunt. That was good: creaking ox-drawn wagons; smells of
smoke, roasting meat, live horseflesh, fellowmen's sweat, dung
and piss, *closeness* within the huge grass-rippling horizon, beneath huge hawk-haunted heaven; noise, laughter, gluttonous
eating; after nightfall, gatherings about the fires, flames whirling
and crackling aloft, picking the faces of trusty friends out of unrestful shadows; talk, perhaps thoughtful or perhaps bragging,
maybe a lay of heroic times to inspire the young, ancient times
when the Middle Kingdom itself feared the Hunnish Empire,
or maybe a jolly bawdy song howled forth to the thutter of drums
and tweedle of flutes while men stamped a ring-dance; and
kumiss, bowl after bowl of rich fermented mare's milk until a
man became a stallion and sought his yurt and his women. . . .
Yes, barring lightning storms (Uldin made a hasty sign against
demons, taught him by the shaman at his initiation), summer
was good, and to arrive home now would be to have a foretaste of
it.

However, no softness could be allowed. It was bad for discipline if nothing else, and what was a tribe without discipline?
Uldin drew from beneath his saddlegirth the tally stick on which
he had recorded the size of his flocks, and made a show of study-
ing it.

Not small. Nor big. He was no clan chief, just the head of a
household, so-and-so many younger sons and the like who had
given him their pledge, together with their dependents and his
own children, wives, concubines, hirelings, slaves, horses, cattle,
sheep, dogs, wagons, gear, and plunder.

Plunder. He had won little of that when the Huns were overrunning the Alans east of the Don River, for in those years he
was but a youth learning the trade of war. The sack of the

Gothic holdings had enriched him somewhat. Now, when graz-
ing had been made ample, he would do best to trade silver and
silks for livestock and let natural increase bring him the only
wealth that was really real.

But his gaze drifted westward. Beyond this rolling plain, he
had heard, were mountains, and beyond the mountains were the
Romans, and it was said they paved their streets with gold. A
man might carve himself an empire there, great as the ancestors',
so that folk a thousand years hence would tremble at his name.

No, that chance would hardly come in Uldin's lifetime. The
Huns had no reason to conquer further nor would until their
numbers waxed too large. To be sure, without some battle the
skills of war would rust and the tribes become easy prey; hence
the West Goths and others would at least be raided pretty often,
which could bring opportunities.

Abide, he told himself. Honor the Powers and the ancestors,
stand by your Shanyu and do his will as you expect your household to do yours, steer your affairs wisely. Then who knows
what may come your way?

And the vortex took him.

Again Erissa must seek the heights alone.

She did not know what sent her forth. It might be the whisper
of the Goddess or, if this was too bold a thought, a lesser Being;
but no vision had ever come to her on those pilgrimages. It might
be nothing deeper than a wish to be, for a while, one with the
moon, with sun, stars, winds, distances, and memories. At such
times the house, Dagonas, yes, even the wide fields and woods
that were hers, even the dear tyranny of her children, became
another slave kennel to escape from. So relentlessly was she
driven that she seldom believed there was nothing of the divine
about it. Surely this was a sacrament she must receive, over and
over, until she was purified for the reunion promised her these
four and twenty years ago.

"Tomorrow dawn I leave," she told Dagonas.

Though he had learned the uselessness of protest, he did answer in his mild way, "Deukalion could well return meanwhile."

For a moment her spirit overflowed and stung her eyes, at thought of the tall sea captain who was her oldest son. He was gone from Malath more than he was on the island; and when home he spent most time with his comely wife and children, or his young male friends, and this was right and natural. But he had come to have so many of his father's looks—

The stinging made her aware, too, of how Dagonas had always been kind to the boy who was not his. Of course, he was honored in having for stepson the child of a god. Nonetheless, his goodness went beyond duty. Erissa smiled and kissed her husband. "If he does, pour him a rhyton of Cyprian wine for me," she said.

Dagonas was eager that night, knowing she would be absent for days. He had never cared for other women. (Well, he must have had them in foreign ports, seeing how long a merchant voyage could become, just as she had taken occasional men in his absence; but after he retired from that life and went into brokerage, it had been entirely they two.) She tried to respond, but her dreams were on Mount Atabyris and a quarter century in the past.

—She woke before the slaves themselves were up. Fumbling her way in the dark, she got a brand from the hearthfire and lit a lamp. When she made her ablutions, the water lashed her blood with cold until it raced. She dressed in proper style before kneeling, signing herself, and saying her prayers at the household shrine. Dagonas had made that image of the Goddess and the Labrys above, with his own clever hands. Cradling Her Son in Her arms, Our Lady of the Ax seemed by the uncertain light to stand alive, stirring, as if Her niche were a window that opened upon enormous reaches.

Religious duties performed, Erissa made ready to travel. She shed long skirt and open-bosomed jacket for a tunic and stout sandals; her hair she wound in a knot; at her belt she hung a knife and a wallet to carry food. She swallowed a piece of bread, a lump of cheese, a cup of mingled wine and water. Softly—no need to rouse them—she stole into the pair of rooms they had and kissed her four living children by Dagonas farewell. Two boys, two girls, ages from seventeen and soon to be a bride (O Virgin Britomartis, her age when the god found her!) to chubby sweet-smelling three. She forgot until she was on her way that she had not saluted her man.

Westward a few stars still glimmered in sea-blue depths, but the east was turning white, dew gleamed and birds twittered. Her house was actually not far outside the harbor city; but steeply rising land and dense groves of fig, pomegranate, and olive trees cut off view of anything save her own holdings.

Dagonas had demurred when she chose the site: "Best we live in town, behind its walls. Each year sees more pirates. Here we would have none to help defend us."

She had laughed, not merrily but with that bleak noise which ended argument, and replied, "After what we have lived through, my dear, are we afraid of a few curs?"

Later, because he was no weakling, no mainlander who could not cope with a woman unless he had a law making her inferior, she explained, "We'll build the house stoutly and hire only men who can fight. Thus we can stand off any attack long enough for a smoke signal to fetch help. I do need broad acres around me, if I'm to breed the sacred bulls."

Having left the buildings behind and taken an inland trail, she passed one of the meadows where her cattle dwelt. The cows drowsed in mist-steaming grass or stood with calves clumsily butting their udders. The Father of Minotaurs was also on his feet, beneath a plane tree whose upper leaves snared the first beams of the unseen sun. She stopped a moment, caught on the grandeur of his horns. His coat was softly dappled, like shadows on a forest floor, and beneath it his muscles moved like a calm sea. Oh, holy! The wish to dance with him was an ache within her.

No. The god who fathered Deukalion had thereby taken away her right to do it in Her honor; and time, slowing her down, had taken away her right as wife and mother to do it for the instruction of the young.

Otherwise she had lost little from her body. Pebbles scrunched beneath her mile-eating stride.

A swineherd, further on where the unpeopled lands began, recognized her and bent the knee. She blessed him but did not pause. Strictly speaking, she was not entitled to do that. She was no priestess, simply a wise-woman, skilled in the healing arts, in soothsaying, and in beneficent magic. This let her behave as she chose—faring off by herself, clad like a mainlander man—without unduly shocking respectable folk; but it did not consecrate her.

Yet a wise-woman must needs be close to the divine; and Erissa had taken the lead in restoring certain forms of worship among the Malathians; and she had herself, when a maiden, danced with the bulls for Our Lady; and, while she made no point of having once been chosen by a god, neither did she make any bones about it, and most people believed her. Thus she was no common witch.

The awe of her, waxing over the years, helped Dagonas in his business. Erissa grinned.

Her muscles flexed and eased, flexed and eased, driving her always further inland and upward. Before long she was in ancient pine forest. At that height, under those scented boughs, the coolness of autumn began to grow chilly. She took her noontide meal beside a rushing brook. It widened into a pool where she could have handcaught a fish to eat raw, were she not bound for a shrine of the Goddess and therefore prohibited from killing.

She reached her goal at dusk: a cave high in the highest mountain on Malath. In a hut nearby dwelt the sibyl. Erissa made her offering, a pendant of Northland amber which enclosed for eternity a beetle. The Egyptian sign being very potent, that was a valuable donation. Hence the sibyl not only gave Erissa routine leave to pray before the three images at the front of the cave—Britomartis the Maiden, Rhea the Mother, Dictynna the Rememberer and Foreseer—but led her past the curtain to the spring and its Mystery.

The hut was well stocked with food brought up by country-folk. After they had eaten, the sibyl wanted to gossip, but Erissa was in no mood for it and, because she too had powers, could scarcely be compelled. They went early to bed.

—Erissa was likewise up betimes, and on the mountaintop shortly after daybreak.

Here, alone in stillness and splendor, she could let go her tears.

Beneath her the slopes fell away in crags, cliffs, boulders, stone strong and dark against the green of pines, which finally gave place to the many-hued fields and orchards of men. Overhead the sky soared altogether clear, holding an eagle whose wings sheened gold in the young light of Asterion, the sun, the Son. The air was cool, pungent with sage and thyme, and cast a breeze to lift the hair off a wet brow. Around the island reached the sea, blue and green shading afar to purple, streaked with a dazzlement of foam. Northwestward, fellow islands stood like white-hulled ships; northward reared Asia, still hazy with night dreams. But southward hung the peak of Mount Ida, where Asterion was born, upon Keft the lovely and forever lost.

There was no sign of Kharia-ti-yeh. There would never be again in the world.

"God Duncan," Erissa wept, raising to heaven a hand that gripped a piece of earth, "when will you call me back to you?"

And the vortex took her.

They stood in a land that the sun had burnt barren. On brown rock-strewn ground, scored by gullies, grew scattered thornbushes. Heat shimmers danced on the southern horizon. To north the desert met waters that shone like whetted metal beneath an unmerciful glare and three wheeling vultures.

They looked upon the land and upon each other. They screamed.

# THREE

IN THE INSTANT beyond time when he was seized and borne off, Reid's terror cried out: Oh, no! Not a stroke—this soon in my life! Then he stumbled back from the desolation that filled eyes, ears, lungs; but it was everywhere around him, it had him. The words flashed through: I'm dreaming. I'm delirious. I'm dead and in hell.

A wind boomed, mummy dry, furnace hot, hissing with grit that whipped his skin.

The voices pierced his own and brought him jerkily about. Three! A yellow-bearded man in spike-topped helmet and chainmail; a short, leather-coated, fur-capped rider on a rearing pony; a tall, slender woman in a knee-length white dress. And Duncan Reid. They shuddered, twenty or thirty feet apart and equally distant from the thing that lay motionless.

Thing . . . a tapered cylindroid, ten yards long by four yards maximum radius or thereabouts, coppery-shining and featureless. Or was it? An iridescent shimmer played in the air immediately over the surface, making the very shape impossible to tell with certainty.

The horseman got his mount under control. At once he snatched a double-curved bow that hung at his saddle, an arrow from the quiver beside, and had the weapon strung and armed. The blond man roared and lifted an ax. The woman drew a knife of reddish metal. Reid struggled to wake from this nightmare. A fraction of him noticed how his legs tensed to run.

But then the woman's frantically flickering glance reached him. She uttered a new shriek, not of terror but—what?—and dropped her blade and sped toward him.

"Hey!" Reid heard himself croak, weakly and ridiculously. "I, I don't know—who are you? Where are we?"

She reached him, she flung arms about him, her mouth met his in a fierceness to break lips open against teeth. He lurched, almost falling. Her tears washed away the blood and trickled saltily onto his tongue. She kept sobbing words he could not follow except that he thought his name was among them, which was the final insanity. After a moment, when he had not returned her embrace or her kiss, she went to her knees. Her hair, fallen loose from a knot, hid her lowered countenance in midnight waves.

Reid gaped toward the others. They stared back. The sight of him and her thus together must have eased them the least bit, made them suppose this might not be a death trap. The bearded man lowered his ax, the rider stopped pointing his arrow at anyone in particular.

Silence, except for the wind and the weeping.

Reid drew three deep breaths. His pulse still racketed but was slowing; he no longer trembled. And he could think. That alone was a deliverance.

His senses had become preternaturally keen in the unknownness that poured through them. His cooling brain began to catalogue the data. Dry heat; sun high in a cloudless brazen vault; baked soil where a few scrubby bushes and tufts of harsh grass survived; blowing dust; not far away, a sea or giant lake. Every detail was strange to him, but every detail was there.

The same was true of the woman at his feet. He saw that her garment appeared to be homespun and that its blue border appeared to be vegetable dye. He saw that her sandals were stitched and had nothing but leather in them, being secured by straps tied halfway up the calf. He saw the smears of local dirt, and traces of older stains that any commercial bleach ought to have removed. She clasped his shoes. He felt the touch and noticed that her hands and feet were large but beautifully shaped, that the nails were pared short and carried no sign of polish, that her left wrist bore a wide silver bracelet studded with turquoises which was not Navajo work.

He could recall no dream so complete, dustgrain by dustgrain. And things held steady. He returned his gaze to a tussock and it had not become a toadstool. Events weren't telescoped, either; they happened second by second, each instant a logical continuation of the last.

Real time?

Could you dream you were dreaming a real-time dream?

Whatever was happening, he didn't see how he could lose by doing what was rational. He lifted his hands, palms outward, and forced himself to smile at the two men.

The fellow in armor did not exactly reply in kind, but he scowled less hard and walked closer. He held his ax slantwise before him, gauntleted hands well apart on the long shaft. When he halted, a couple of yards from Reid, he stood with knees slightly bent and feet at right angles. The architect thought: He's not an actor. He knows how to use that thing. Otherwise he'd take a woodchopper stance, like me before I saw his. And his weapon's been in service, too—that nick in the edge, that scratch in the blade.

Where have I seen this kind of battle ax before?

A chill flew up and down his spine: Axes quite like it on the Bayeux Tapestry, carried by the English at Hastings.

The man growled what must be a string of questions. His language was as alien as the woman's—no, not quite; it had a spooky half-familiarity, must be related to one Reid had heard in foreign movies or while serving his hitch in Europe. The man made a truculent jerk of his head back toward the coppery object.

Reid's mouth was too parched for him to talk other than huskily: "Sorry. I . . . I'm a stranger here myself. Do you speak English? *Parlez-vous français? ¿Habla usted español? Sprechen Sie Deutsch?*" Those were the tongues in which he had a few phrases. They got no response.

However, the man seemed to understand that Reid too was

a victim. He slapped his broad chest and said, "Oleg Vladimirovitch Novgorodna." After several repetitions, Reid caught
the syllables.

It rocked him. "*R-r-russki?*" he stammered. Again persistence
was needed to get past the barriers of accent.

Oleg nodded. "*Da, ya yest Novgorodni. Podvlastni Knyaza
Yaroslava.*"

Reid shook his head, baffled. "*Sovietski?*" he ventured. Oleg
tried to answer and gave up. Reid stooped past the woman, who
had assumed a watchful crouch, and drew in the sand *CCCP.*
He threw Oleg an inquiring lift of eyebrows. Everybody knew
that much Cyrillic; it answered to USSR, and the Soviets
claimed nearly one hundred percent literacy. But Oleg shrugged
and flung his arms wide in a purely Slavic gesture.

The American rose. They peered at each other.

Oleg's outfit had been too strange for the human to show
through until now. His helmet, conical and rising in a spike,
sat atop a padded cloth coif on which, between rim and shoulders, were sewn small rings. The sleeveless hauberk was made
of larger rings, interlocked, falling almost to the knees. It likewise had a quilted undergarment, above a white linen shirt. That
must be murderous here; the black iron was wet with the per-
spiration that ran off its wearer. At a brass-buckled belt were
fastened a dagger and a leather purse. Trousers of coarse blue
linen were tucked into gaily red and green boots. The gauntlets
were leather too, strips of brass riveted on their backs.

The man looked thirtyish, about five feet seven or eight, tre-
mendously wide and muscular. A slight paunch and jowliness
didn't lower the impression of bear strength. His head and face
were round, snub-nosed, mustached, dense golden beard cropped
under the jaw. Against the redness of a skin long exposed to
weather, beneath shaggy yellow brows, his eyes were china blue.

"You . . . seem to be . . . a decent guy," Reid said, knowing
how foolish he was.

Oleg pointed at him, obviously demanding his name. The
recollection of his chat with engineer Stockton—Christ almighty,

half an hour ago in the middle of an ocean!—smote Reid like a physical blow. He staggered. The world spun around him. "Duncan," he mumbled.

"Duncan!" The woman leaped up and sprang to him. He leaned on her till things steadied. "Duncan," she crooned, half laughing, half crying, "*ka ankhash* Duncan."

A shadow fell across them. Oleg bounced into battle posture. The horseman had joined their group. His bow was taut and his expression mean.

Somehow that rallied Reid. "Take it easy, friend," he said, uselessly except for the tone, the smile, the palms lifted in peace. "We're not conspiring against you." He tapped his chest, gave his name, did likewise for Oleg. Before he could ask of the woman, whom he finally noticed was more than handsome, she said, "Erissa," like a challenge.

The mounted man considered them.

Neither he nor his steed was prepossessing. The pony was a mustang type—no, not with that blocky head; rather, it resembled the tarpan of central Asia—dun-colored, shaggy, mane and tail braided, blue tassels woven in: an entire male, doubtless fast and tough but no show animal. It was unshod, its bridle of primitive design, saddle high-peaked fore and aft and short in the stirrups. From that saddle hung a full quiver, a lariat, a greasy felt bag, and a leather bottle.

The rider wore clumsy felt-soled shoes; full trousers of rough gray cloth, tied at the ankles, unbelievably dirty; a felt shirt which could be smelled ten feet off; a long leather coat, belted at the waist; and a round fur cap. For cutlery he had a knife and a kind of saber.

He was powerfully built but dwarfish, five feet three or so, bandy-legged, hairy except for the head. That was shaven, Reid learned afterward, leaving a single black tuft on top and behind either golden-ringed ear. The face was so hideously scarred that scant beard grew. Those cicatrices must have been made deliberately, since they formed looping patterns. Beneath them, the features were heavy, big hook nose and flaring nostrils, thick lips, high cheekbones, sloping forehead, slitted eyes. The skin was a weatherbeaten olive, the whole effect more Armenian or Turkish than Mongol.

Oleg had been rumbling in his whiskers. *"Nye Pecheneg,"* he decided, and snapped: *"Polovtsi? Bolgarni?"*

The rider took aim. Reid saw his bow was compound, of laminated horn, and remembered reading that a fifty-pound draw would send an arrow through most armor. "Hey!" he exclaimed. "Easy!" When the horseman glowered at him, he repeated the introductions; then, pointing to the shimmering cylinder, he acted out his bewilderment and motioned to include Oleg and Erissa.

The rider made up his mind to cooperate. "Uldin, *chki ata* Günchên," he said. "Uldin. Uldin." Stabbing a begrimed fingernail from one to the next, he worked on their names till he had those straight. Finally he indicated himself again—all the while keeping his bow handy—and uttered a row of gutturals.

Oleg caught the idea first. He made the same gesture. "Oleg Vladimirovitch," he said. "Novgorodski." He pointed and questioned: "Duncan?"

Who are you? Not you personally; what people do you belong to? That must be it. "Duncan Reid. American." They were as bemused as everyone else was by Erissa's "Keftiu."

For her part, she seemed astonished and hurt that Reid was not more responsive to her. She slipped off to recover her knife. He recognized the metal as bronze. And the iron of yonder arrowhead was precisely that, wrought iron; and Oleg's equipment was either plain iron too or low-carbon steel, and when you looked closely you saw that each ring, each rivet had been individually forged.

And at the end of a sentence, Uldin was saying of himself, "—Hun."

He did not pronounce the word in Anglo-Saxon wise, but it rammed into Reid. "Hun?" he gulped. Uldin nodded, with a wintry grin. "At—Attila?" That drew blank; and, while Oleg tugged his beard and appeared to be searching his memory, the name clearly had no deep significance for him, and none for Erissa.

A Russian who felt his nationality was less important than the fact he hailed from Novgorod; a Hun to whom Attila meant nothing; a Keftiu, whatever that was, whose gaze lay with troubled adoration on . . . on an American, snatched from the North Pacific Ocean to a desert shore where nobody else had ever heard of America. . . . The answer began to break on Reid.

It couldn't be true. It mustn't be.

Because Erissa was nearest, he reached toward her. She took both his hands. He felt how she shivered.

She stood a bare three inches under him, which made her towering if she belonged to the Mediterranean race that her looks otherwise bespoke. She was lean, though full enough in hips and firm breasts to please any man, and long-limbed, swan-necked, head proudly held. That head was dolichocephalic but wide across brow and cheeks, tapering toward the chin, with a classically straight nose and a full and mobile mouth which was a touch too big for conventional beauty. Arching brows and sooty lashes framed large bright eyes whose hazel shifted momentarily from leaf-green to storm-gray. Her black hair, thick and wavy, fell past her shoulders; a white streak ran back from the forehead. Except for suntan, a dusting of freckles, a few fine wrinkles and crow's-feet, a beginning dryness, her skin was clear and fair. He guessed her age as about equal to his.

But she walked like a girl, no, like a danseuse, like a Danilova, a Fonteyn, a Tallchief, a leopard.

His smile wavered forth anew. She put aside both her trouble and her worship and smiled shyly in return.

"Ah-hmph!" Oleg said. Reid released Erissa, clasped hands with the Russian, and offered a shake to the Hun who, after a second, accepted. He urged them by gestures to do the same among each other.

"Fellowship," he declaimed, because any human sound was good in this wasteland. "We're caught in some unbelievable accident, we want home again, okay, we stick together. Right?"

He looked at the cylinder. A minute passed while he mustered courage. The wind blew, his heart knocked. "That thing brought us," he said, and started toward it.

They hesitated. He waved them to come along. Erissa soared in his direction. He made her follow behind. Oleg muttered what was probably a curse and joined her. He seemed about ready to collapse in a pool of sweat. Uldin advanced too, but further back. Reid guessed the Hun was a pro, more interested in being able to cover a wide field with his archery than in heroics. Not that Oleg was equipped for anything but close-in fighting.

Beneath Reid's shoes, dirt and gravel scrunched. His topcoat was smothering him. He took it off and, thinking about possible sunstroke, draped it on his head for a crude burnoose. The hollow-voiced wind tried to blow it away. Behind the cylindroid, barrenness reached on, and on, and on, till horizon met sky in a vague blur of mirages and dust devils. The cylindroid was almost as hard to make out, within the shifting mother-of-pearl light-mist that enveloped it.

That's a machine, though, he compelled himself to understand. And I, the only child here of a machine age, I am the only one who has a chance to deal with it.

How big a chance?

Bitsy. Pam. Mark. Tom. Dad. Mother. Sisters, brothers. Phil Meyer and our partnership. Seattle, the Sound, the Straits, the wooded islands, the mountains behind; Vancouver; funny old Victoria; the Golden Gate Bridge, upward leap of walls from the Rotterdam waterfront, Salisbury Cathedral, half-timbered steep-gabled delight of Riquewihr, a thatch-roofed hut in a Hokusai print and those homes you were going to build; why does a man never know how much there was in his world before he stands at the doors of death?

Pam, Pamela, Pamlet as I called you for a while, will you remember that underneath everything I loved you?

Is that true, or am I just posturing for myself?

No matter. I'm almost at the machine.

The time machine?

Nonsense. A bilgeful of crap. Physical, mathematical, logical impossibility. I proved it once, for a term paper in the philosophy of science.

I, who recall well how it felt to be that confidently analytical twenty-year-old, now know how it feels to be marooned without warning in a grisly desert, nearing a machine like none I had imagined, at my back a medieval Russian and a Hun from before Attila and a woman from no place or age bespoken in any of the books I read when I might have been being kind to Pamela.

Abruptly the iridescence whirled, became a maelstrom, focused its shiningness upon a single point of the metal thing. That point grew outward, opened as a circle, gave onto a dusk-purple space within where twinkled starry sparks of light. A man came forth.

Reid had an instant to see him. He was small, compactly built, mahogany in hue, hair a cap of black velvet, features broad but finely molded. He wore a prismatic white robe and transparent boots. In his hands he bore twin two-foot hemispheres of bright metal upon which were several tiny studs, plates, and switches.

He walked uncertainly, he looked very ill, and his garb was discolored by vomit stains.

Reid halted. "Sir—" he began, making the sign of peace.

The man reeled and fell. Blood ran from his mouth and nostrils. The dust quickly drank it. Behind him, the portal closed.

# FOUR

"My god! If the pilot's dead!" Down on his knees, Reid felt across the still body. The rib cage moved, though with unhealthy rapidity and shallowness. The skin was hotter than the desert beneath.

Erissa joined him. Her face had gone utterly intent. Murmuring to herself what sounded like an invocation, she examined the dark man with unmistakable skill: peeling back a lid to study the pupil, timing his pulse against her rhythmic chant, pulling the robe around his shoulders and cutting off the form-fitting undergarment to check for broken bones or flesh injuries. The hale men waited anxiously. She rose, glanced about, pointed toward a ravine.

"Yeah, get him out of the sun," Reid interpreted. "Us too." He remembered he was not among English speakers. But they caught the idea. Oleg gave Erissa his ax, took the pilot, and bore him easily off. She pulled an amulet from below her tunic, a gold miniature suspended on a thong around her neck, and touched it to the weapon before carrying that with some reverence after the Russian.

Reid tried to study the cylindroid. At a distance of a few feet, where the nacreous flickering began, he was stopped. It was like walking into an invisible rubber sheet, that yielded at first but increased resistance inch by inch. Protective force field, he thought. Not an overwhelming surprise in the present context. Better stay clear—possible radiation hazard—m-m, probably not, since the pilot—but how do we get in?

We don't, without him.

Reid collected the hemispheres. Their hollow interiors were more elaborate than the exterior shells. The only comprehensible features were triads of crisscrossing bands, suggestive of helmet liner suspensions. Were these, then, communication devices to be worn on the head? He carried them along to the gulch. On the way, he noticed the pipe that had fallen from his mouth and retrieved it. Even on doomsday, you find trivia to take care of.

Steep-sided, the ravine gave shelter from the wind and a few patches of shade. Oleg had stretched the pilot—as Reid thought of the unconscious man—in the largest of these. It was inadequate. Reid and Erissa worked together, cutting sticks and propping them erect to support an awning made of his topcoat. Oleg shed armor and pads, heaving a gigantic sigh of relief. Uldin took the harness off his horse, tethered it to a grass tuft above the gulch, and covered the beast as well as he could with the unfolded saddle blanket. He brought bag and bottle down and shared the contents. Nobody had appetite for the dried meat in the first; but sour and alcoholic though it was, the milky liquid in the second proved a lifesaver.

Then they could do nothing but squat in their separate bits of shadow and endure. Erissa went often to check on the pilot. Oleg and Uldin climbed the crumbly bank by turns, peered through a full circle, and returned shaking their heads. Reid sat amidst thoughts that he never quite recalled later except for his awareness of Erissa's eyes dwelling on him.

Whatever was happening, he could no longer pretend he'd soon awaken from it.

The sun trudged westward. Shadows in the ravine stretched and flowed together. The four who waited lifted faces streaked with dust and sweat-salt, reddened eyes and cracked gummy lips, toward the first faint balm of coolness.

The pilot stirred and called out. They ran to him.

He threshed his limbs and struggled to sit. Erissa tried to make him lie down. He would not. "*Mentatór*," he kept gasping, and more words in a language that sounded faintly Hispanic but was softer. He retched. His nosebleed broke out afresh. Erissa stanched it with a piece torn off a handkerchief Reid had given her. She signed Oleg to uphold him in a reclining posture and herself helped him drink a little of the stuff Uldin called kumiss.

"Wait a minute." Reid trotted back to where he had huddled and fetched the hemispheres. The pilot nodded with a weak vehemence that made Erissa frown, and reached shakily for them. When Reid hunkered to assist him, she stepped aside, clearly setting the American's judgment above her own.

Damn if I know whether I'm doing right, he thought. This guy looks barely alive, on fire with fever, shouldn't be put to any strain. But if he can't get back into his machine, we may all be finished.

The pilot made fumbling adjustments to the devices. He put one on his head. The shining metal curve turned his sunken-eyed, blood-crusted, dirt-smudged countenance doubly ghastly. He leaned back on Oleg's breast and signed Reid to don the second helmet. The American obeyed. The pilot had barely strength to reach and press a stud on his. It was the most prominent, directly over his brow. The hand fell into his lap; but fingers fluttered at Reid.

The architect rallied what guts he had left. Be ready for anything, he told himself, and tough it out, son, tough it out. He pushed the control.

A humming grew. The noise must be inside his skull, for none of the others heard; and somehow it didn't feel physical, not like anything carried along the nerves. He grew dizzy and sat down. But that might be only from tension, on top of these past dreadful hours.

The pilot was in worse case. He twitched, whimpered, closed his eyes and sagged bonelessly. It was as if his machine were a vampire draining his last life. Erissa ventured to kneel by him, though not to interrupt.

After what Reid's watch said was about five minutes, the humming faded out. The depressed studs popped up. The giddiness passed away. Presumably the helmets had finished their job. The pilot lay half conscious. When Reid took off his headpiece, Erissa removed that of her patient and laid him flat. She stayed beside him, listened to the struggling breath and watched the uncertain pulse in his throat.

Finally he opened his eyes. He whispered. Erissa brought her ear close, frowned, and waved at Reid. He didn't know what he could do, but joined her anyway. The pilot's dim glance fell upon him and remained there.

"Who . . . are you?" rattled from the parched mouth. "Where, when . . . are you from?"

American English!

"Quick," pleaded the voice. "Haven't . . . got long. For your sake too. You know . . . *mentatór?* This device?"

"No," Reid answered in awe. "Language teacher?"

"Right. Scan speech center. In the brain. Brain's a data bank. The scanner . . . retrieves language information . . . feeds it into the receiver brain. Harmless, except it's . . . kind of stressful . . . being the receiver . . . seeing as how then the data patterns aren't just scanned, they're imposed."

"You should have let me learn yours, then."

"No. Too confusing. You wouldn't know how to use . . . too many of the concepts. Teach that scar-faced savage over there words like . . . like 'steam engine' . . . and you still couldn't talk to him for days, weeks, till he'd digested the idea. About steam engines, I mean. But you two could . . . get together at once . . . on horses." The pilot paused for breath. "I haven't got that kind of time to spare."

In the background Oleg was crossing himself, right to left, and muttering Russian prayers. Uldin had scrambled to a distance, where he made gestures that must be against black magic. Erissa held firm by Reid, though she touched her amulet to her lips. He saw, surprised at noticing, that it had the form of a double-bitted ax.

"You're from the future, aren't you?" Reid asked.

A wraith of a smile passed over the pilot's mouth. "We all are. I'm Sahir. Of the . . . I don't remember what the base date of your calendar was. Is. Will be. I started from . . . yes, Hawaii . . . in the . . . *anakro*—call it a space-time vehicle. Pass over Earth's surface, or waters, while traveling through time. We were bound for . . . prehistoric Africa. Protoman. We're . . . we were . . . anthropologists, I guess, comes closest. Could I have some more to drink?"

"Sure." Reid and Erissa helped him.

"Ahh!" Sahir lay back. "I feel a little stronger. It won't last. I'd better talk while I can. Figured you're postindustrial, you. Makes a difference. Identify yourself?"

"Duncan Reid, American, from 1970—latter twentieth century—well, we'd lately made the first Lunar landings, and we'd had atomic energy for, uh, twenty-five years—"

"So. I see. Shortly before the Age of—No, I shouldn't say. You might get back. Will, if I can help it. You'd not like to know what's coming. I'm terribly sorry about this mess. Who're your friends?"

"The blond man's early Russian, I think. The short man says he's a Hun—I think. The woman here . . . I can't figure her out."

"Hm. Yes. We can get—you can get—closer information after using the *mentatór*. The helmets are set for scan and imprint. Make sure which is which.

"Listen, pick whoever's from the most ancient period—looks like that'll be her—make her supply your common language. Most useful one, you see? We're only a short ways back in time and south in space from . . . the point . . . where the machine sucked in the last person. I'd nearly gotten it braked . . . by then.

"Early model. S'posed to be insulated . . . against energy effects. Takes immense energy concentration to warp the continuum. For returning home . . . would've assembled the nuclear generator we carry . . . outside the vessel, of course, because the energy release's in the megaton range. . . ."

Sahir plucked at his robe. His head rolled, as did his eyes within their sockets. His voice was nearly inaudible, the momentary strength running out of him like wine from a broken cup; but he whispered in pathetic haste:

"Warp fields . . . s'posed to be contained, controlled, not interact with matter en route . . . but defect here. Defect. Soon after we started, instruments mentated to us that we'd drawn a body along. I ordered a halt right away . . . but inertia—We c'lected higher animals only, men, horse, 'cause control, instrumentation, everything mentated. . . . And then we passed too close in space-time to—to some monstrous energy release, I don't know what, terrible catastrophe in this far past. Course was pre-set, y' get me? We were s'posed to pass by—for a boost—but we were leaving the whole job to the computer. . . . Now, when we'd nearly stopped . . . faulty insulation, did I tell you? Interaction with our warp fields. Blew out our interior power cybernets. Radiation blast—s'prised I'm still alive—partner's dead—knocked me out for a while—I came to, figured I'd go meet you, but—"

Sahir tried to lift his hands. Reid took them. It was like holding smoldering parchment. "Listen," Sahir susurrated desperately. "That . . . blowup, crash, whatever it is . . . in this part of the world. Near future. Year or less. Listen. There aren't . . . won't be . . . many time expeditions. Ever. Energy cost too great . . . and . . . environment couldn't stand much of that. . . . But anything this big, bound t' be observers. Understand? You find 'em, identify yourself, get help—maybe for me too—"

"How?" Reid choked.

"First . . . get me to vehicle. It's wrecked, but . . . medical supplies. . . . They'll come through time, to this day, bring help, surely—" Sahir jerked as if a lightning bolt coursed through him. "*Nia!*" he screamed. "*Fabór, Teo, nia, nia!*"

He crumpled. His eyeballs rolled back, his jaw dropped. Reid attempted mouth-to-mouth resuscitation and chest massage. They were of no use.


# FIVE


NIGHT BROUGHT cold air and brilliant stars. The sea glimmered vaguely. It was without surf or tides, but wavelets chuckled against the stones of the beach. The land reared and rolled southward, a blackness where hills stood humpbacked athwart the constellations and yelps resounded which Reid guessed were from jackals.

He had considered gathering brush for a fire, after Sahir was laid in a gully and covered with clods and rocks for lack of grave-digging tools. His pipe lighter would kindle it. Uldin, assuming they must go through the laborious use of the flint and steel he carried, spoke against the idea. "No need. You and I have coats, Oleg has his padding, I can lend Erissa my saddle blanket. And the . . . shaman wagon . . . it shines, no? Why wear ourselves out scratching around for sticks?"

"Water nearby will keep the air from growing too chill," Oleg pointed out from the experience of a sailor.

Reid decided to save his lighter fluid for emergencies, or for what tobacco was in his pouch, though he dared not smoke until he had an abundance to drink.

The sea—definitely a sea, salt as it was—would help a trifle. He'd read Alain Bombard's report; you can keep alive awhile by taking continual sips. And they might try for fish with whatever tackle they could rig. In the long run, however, and not a terribly long run either, nothing would save them but rescue from outside.

The glow enclosing the time vessel swirled in soft white and pastels, a hateful loveliness that barred off the water, food, shelter, medicine, tools, weapons within. It lit the desert wanly for some yards around. Sahir had known how to unlock it; but Sahir lay stiff awaiting the jackals. Reid felt sorry for him, who had been a well-intentioned man and wanted to live as badly as anyone, and sorry likewise for the partner whose ray-raddled flesh sprawled in the machine that had betrayed them all. But his pity was abstract. He'd never known them as people. He himself, and these three with him, remained to be saved or to die a harder death.

Oleg yawned cavernously. "Woof, what a day! Are we lost in time as you believe, Duncan, or borne off by evil Lyeshy as I think? Either way, I'm for sleep. Maybe I'll have such pious dreams the angels will carry me back to my little wife."

"Do you want the second or third watch, then?" Uldin asked.

"None. I sleep in my mail, helmet and ax to hand. What use, seeing an enemy from afar?"

"To make ready for him, you lump, or find a hiding place if he's too strong," Uldin snapped. Dirt, grease, stink, scars, and everything, the Hun nonetheless reminded Reid of a martinet captain he'd had. The Russian growled but yielded.

"Let me take first watch," Reid offered. "I can't sleep yet anyway."

"You think too much," Uldin grunted. "It weakens a man. As you will, though. You, next me, last Oleg."

"What of me?" Erissa inquired.

Uldin's look told his opinion of putting a woman on sentry-go. He walked from the illumination and studied the heavens. "Not my sky," he said. "I can name you the northerly stars, but something's queer about them. Well, Duncan, do you see that bright one low in the east? Call me when it's this high." He doubtless had no idea of geometry, but his arm lifted to an accurate sixty-degree angle. With his awkward gait, he sought the spot where his horse was tethered, lay down, and slumbered immediately.

Oleg knelt, removed his coif, and crossed himself before saying a prayer in his Old Russian. He had no trouble finding rest either.

I envy them that, Reid thought. Intelligence—no, don't be snobbish—the habit of verbalizing has its drawbacks.

Weariness filled his body with stones and his head with sand. Most of Uldin's kumiss had gone to wash down the jerky they had for supper; what was left must be hoarded; Reid's mouth felt drier than deadwood. His skin was flushed from the day's exposure, yet the cold gnawed into him. A brisk walk, several times around the camp, might help.

"I leave, Duncan, soon to return," Erissa said.

"Don't go far," he warned.

"No. Never from you."

He waited till she had vanished in the night before he started on his round, so he could watch her. Not that he felt enamored

—under these circumstances?—but what a woman she was, and what a mystery.

The castaways had had slim chance to talk. The shock of arrival and of Sahir's appearance and death, the stress of heat, thirst, and language transfer, had overtaxed them. They were lucky to complete what they did before sunset.

Reid had followed the pilot's advice. Because her bronze knife and her frank wonder at iron equipment fairly well proved she was from the earliest date and therefore from this general period, he made Erissa the linguistic source. She went along with the process as readily as with anything he wanted. He found that assimilating a language through the *mentatór* was in truth rough: a churning of his mind, bringing on a condition similar to the unpleasant terminal stage of extreme drunkenness, plus exhausting, involuntary muscle contractions. No doubt it went far more slowly and gently in Sahir's home milieu; and obviously this brutal cramming had hastened the pilot's end. But there was no choice and Reid recovered after a drowsy rest.

Oleg and Uldin refused, wouldn't come near the apparatus, until the Russian saw Erissa and the American talking freely. Then he put a helmet on his own pate. Uldin followed suit, maybe just to show that he had equal manhood.

The swift desert dark upon them and their vitality drained, they had no time thereafter for aught but the briefest, most general exchanges of information.

Reid started pacing. The crunch of his footfalls and the remote bestial yelps were his sole hearing, the stars and the cold his sole attendants. He doubted there would be any danger before morning. Still, Uldin was right about posting a guard. Heavy though Reid's brain was, it lurched into motion.

Where are we? *When* are we?

Sahir's expedition left Hawaii in . . . sometime in the future, Reid thought. Say a thousand years in my future. Their machine skimmed the land and water surface of the planet while moving backward in time.

Why skim? Well, let's assume you need the surface for a

reference frame. Earth moves through space, and space has no absolute coordinates. Let's assume you dare not rise lest you lose your contact (gravitation?) and come out in the emptiness between yonder stars.

My term paper—$x$ millennia hence, a couple of decades ago along my now doubled-back world line, a million years ago in my interior time of this night of despair—proved that travel into the past is impossible for a number of reasons, including the fact that more than infinite energy would be required. Evidently I was wrong. Evidently sufficient energy—a huge concentration of it in a small volume and short timespan—nevertheless, a finite amount—evidently that will, somehow, affect the parameters of the continuum, and this vehicle here can be thrown . . . across the world and backward or forward through the ages.

Traveling, the vehicle must be charged with monstrous forces. Sahir spoke of "insulation." I think he might better have said "control" or "restraint." Probably the forces themselves are the only ones strong enough to generate their own containment.

This trip, there was an imperfection. A leakage. The vehicle flew through space-time surrounded by a . . . field . . . that snatched along whatever animal was encountered.

Why just animals—higher animals—plus whatever was intimately attached to them such as clothes? Why not trees, rocks, water, air, soil? M-m, yes, Sahir did speak of the reason. It wasn't important for me to know, he was half out of his mind and babbling, but as long as he did mention it—Yes. The technology of his age, or at least of its space-time vehicles, relies on mental control. Telepathy, including telepathic robots, if you believe in that kind of fable. Myself, I'm inclined to speculate about amplified neural currents. Whatever the explanation may be, the fact is that the drive field only interacts with matter which is, itself, permeated by brain waves.

It might be done that way as a precaution. Then in case of force leakage, the machine will not find itself buried under tons of stuff when it halts. Higher animals aren't too plentiful, ever. One of them would have to be at precisely the point in space, precisely the instant in time, where-when the vehicle passes by. . . . Hm. We may have collected various mice and birds and whatnot, which hurried out of our sight before we got a chance to notice them. They'd be the commonest victims. An accident involving humans must be rare. Maybe unique.

(Why did it have to happen to me? The eternal question, I suppose, that everybody must sooner or later ask himself.)

Sahir said the trouble registered on instruments and his team started braking. Because of . . . inertia . . . they couldn't stop at the point where they'd picked me up. They flew on, acquiring Oleg, Uldin, and Erissa.

As ill luck would have it, when their flight was nearly ended, when they were nearly ready to halt in space and start moving normally forward again in time—another power concentration hit them. Ordinarily they could have passed it by in safety; but given the faulty containment, those cataclysmic forces (or more accurately, I guess, the space-time warping produced by those cataclysmic forces) interacted with the drive field. Energy was released in the form of a lethal blast of X-rays through the hull.

There's the crazy coincidence, that a time carrier in trouble should happen to pass by a catastrophe.

Uh-uh. Wait. Probably not a coincidence. Probably the chrononauts, or rather their computers and autopilots, always set their courses to pass near events like that if it's feasible. Given a vessel that's working properly, I imagine they get an extra boost from the H-bomb explosion or giant meteorite impact or whatever the event happens to be. Makes the launch cheaper, and so makes more time voyages possible than would otherwise be the case.

Did Sahir and his friend know they were headed into their doom, try to veer, and fail? Or did they forget, in the wild scramble of those few moments? (I have the impression that transit time, experienced within the hull, is short. Certainly we who were carried along outside knew a bare minute's darkness, noise, and whirling.)

So. We're stranded, unless we can find some other futurians.

Or they us. I suppose if we can stay here, eventually a search party will come by.

Will it? How closely can they position their space-time hops, when each requires building a generator that doubtless destroys itself by sheer heat radiation when it's used?

Well, wouldn't the futurians make the effort? If only to be sure that the presence of this wrecked machine doesn't change the past and obliterate them?

Would it do that? *Could* it? This was a point in my essay which may remain valid: that changing the past is a contradiction in terms. "The moving Finger writes, and having writ . . ." I suspect the machine's presence here and now, and ours, are part of what happens. I suspect this night has "always" been.

For what can we do? Chances are we'll die within days. The animals will dispose of our bones. Maybe local tribesmen, if any possess this grim land, will worship the glowing hull for a while. But finally its batteries, or whatever it's got, must run down. The force field will blink out of existence. Unprotected, the metal will corrode away, or be ripped apart for the use of smiths. The fact that a strange thing once lay here will become a folk tale, forgotten in a few generations.

Oh, Pam, what will you think when I never come down to our cabin?

That I fell overboard accidentally? I imagine so. I trust so. Damn, damn, damn, I should've increased my insurance coverage!

"Duncan."

Erissa had come back. Reid glanced at his wristwatch. She'd been gone an hour. Not on an errand of nature, then.

"I was praying," she said simply, "and afterward casting a spell for luck. Though I never doubt you will save us."

In her mouth, the throaty tongue she named Keftiu was softened; she had a low voice and used it gently. Reid had no idea what they called her speech in his era, if they had found any trace of it. His attempts to identify cognates were made extra difficult by the fact that he, like Oleg and Uldin, had actually gained two languages which she spoke with equal fluency, plus smatterings of others.

He knew the term for the second, non-Keftiu tongue, as he knew the term "English" or "*español*." He could pronounce its name, as he could her entire vocabulary from that rather harsh, machine-gun-rapid talk. He could spell the vocabulary; the language had a simplified hieroglyphic-type script, just as Keftiu had a more elaborate and cumbersome written form. But he could not readily transliterate into the Roman alphabet, to compare with words from his own world. Thus his command of the language and his knowledge of its name—*Ah-hyäi-a* was a crude approximation—gave him no clue to the identity of its native speakers.

Since Erissa preferred Keftiu, Reid postponed consideration of the unrelated tongue, however important it probably was in this era. Keftiu was keeping him bemused enough. Though no linguist, he classed it as mainly positional, partly agglutinative, in contrast to its heavily inflected rival.

Perhaps trying to make conversation, she asked him something. Translated more or less literally, her question was, "Of what unknown-to-me nature is that like-unto-Our-Lady's-moon jewel which you (for a sign of Her?) wear?" But his inner ear heard: "Please, what's that? So beautiful, like a sigil of the Goddess."

He showed her the watch. She fingered it reverently. "You didn't have this before," she murmured.

"Before?" He stared at her. The sight was blurry in the dim light, amidst the thick shadows. "You do act as if you already know me," he said slowly.

"But of course! Duncan, Duncan, you cannot have forgotten." She reached from beneath the smelly blanket that, perforce and grimacing, she had wrapped around her tunic. Her fingers brushed his cheek. "Or has the spell fallen on you likewise?" Her head drooped. "The witch made me forget much. You too?"

He jammed hands in coat pockets, clenching a fist around the home shape of his pipe. Breath smoked from him. He begrudged the moisture. "Erissa," he said in his exhaustion, "I don't know any more than you what's happening or has happened. I said what Sahir told me, that we're entangled in time. And that is a terrible thing to be."

"I cannot understand." She shivered where she stood. "You swore we would meet again; but I did not think it would be when a dragon bore me off to a country of death." She straightened. "That's the reason, not so?" she asked with renewed life. "You foresaw this and came to save me who have never stopped loving you."

He sighed. "These are waters too deep to cross before we have even laid our ship's keel," he said, and immediately recognized a Keftiu proverb. "I'm empty. I can't think beyond . . . beyond what few hand-graspable facts we may collect between us."

He paused, groping for words, more because his brain was dull than because there was any great problem about phrasing. "First," he said, "we must know where we are and what year this is."

"What year? Why, it's been four and twenty years, Duncan, since last we were together, you and I, at the wreck of the world."

"At the—what?"

"When the mountain burst and the fires beneath creation raged forth and the sea turned on the Keftiu who were too happy and destroyed them." Erissa lifted her double-ax amulet and signed herself.

The bottom dropped out of Reid's mind. *My God*, gibbered through him, *has the energy release already taken place? Did we arrive after instead of before it? Then we're indeed stuck here forever. Aren't we?*

"You shudder, Duncan." Erissa laid hands on his shoulders. "Come, let me hold you."

"No. I thank you, no." He stood for a while mastering himself.

It could be a misunderstanding. Sahir had been definite about an enormous disaster in this general neighborhood, somewhat futureward of this night. No use trying to untangle the whole skein in an hour. Knot by knot, that was the way. Erissa's home wasn't too distant geographically, was it? Not according to Sahir. Okay, begin with that.

"Tell me," Reid said, "where are you from?"

"What?" She hesitated. "Well . . . I was many places after we parted. I'm now on the island Malath. Before then—oh, many places, Duncan, always longing for the home where you found me."

"The what? Where? Say its name. Where were you then?"

She shook her head. Murky though the night was, he could see her tresses ripple beneath the stars. "You know that, Duncan," she said puzzledly.

"Tell me anyhow," he insisted.

"Why, Kharia-ti-yeh." Land of the Pillar, Reid translated. Erissa went on, anxious to make herself clear in the face of his baffling ignorance: "Or, as they called it on the mainland, Atlantis."

# *SIX*

AWAKENING FROM SLEEP was strange. It locked the final door on escape out of a dream. The twentieth century world had become the one remote, fantastic, not wholly comprehensible as existent.

"I'm going on scout while my horse can serve me," Uldin declared, and took off. He appeared less worn than his companions, maybe because his best appearance was so uncouth. While he was gone, the rest sought refuge in the sea. Sticks, lashed together with thongs cut from Oleg's belt, made a framework on which to hang clothes for protection against direct sunlight and glare reflected off the water in which they would sit to their necks.

When the awning was ready to be positioned, Erissa slipped off sandals and tunic. Oleg gasped. "What's the matter?" she asked him innocently.

"You . . . a woman . . . a, well—" It couldn't be seen whether the Russian blushed under his beet-red sunburn. Suddenly he laughed. "Well, if that's the kind of girl you are, this needn't be the worst day of my life!"

She bridled. "What do you mean? Put down those hands!"

"She's not of your people, Oleg," Reid explained. It was obvious to him: "Among hers, nakedness is respectable." Nevertheless he felt shy about stripping before her. Taut and lithe, scarcely marked by the children she had borne, her body was the goodliest he had ever seen.

"Well, turn your eyes, then, wench, till I've waded out decently deep," Oleg huffed.

Once laved and cooled, they felt better. Even the thirst was easier to bear. Oleg grudgingly imitated Erissa in following Reid's advice about sipping from the sea. "I don't believe, mind you," he said. "It'll kill us off faster in the end. But if we can keep going thus for a while, a bit stronger than otherwise, maybe the saints can find help to send us. You hear me?" he shouted at the sky. "A golden chalice set with precious stones for the Church of St. Boris. Six altar cloths of the finest silk, and scores of pearls sewn on, for St. Mary." He paused. "I'd best say that in Russian and Romaic too. And, oh, yes, Norse."

Reid couldn't resist japing: "Your saints have not been born." Oleg looked stricken. The American added hastily, "Well, I could be wrong, I suppose." No sense in pointing out that Christ—that Abraham, most likely—was also in the future.

He turned to Erissa. "Sleep has cleared my head," he went on. "Let me think hard about what we know." And let me stop being so damned aware of what I glimpse of you through the water, his mind added guiltily.

He made careful inquiries of them both, pausing for long times to ponder. They regarded him with respect. Uldin hadn't shown that; but he had barked curt answers to a few key questions before he left.

Oleg proved a diamond mine of information. Reid decided that the Russian's bluff manner must be in a large part a disarming mask over a sophisticated intelligence. The Kievan state was not the slum that most of its Western contemporaries were. Eight million people dwelt in a territory as big as the United States east of the Mississippi, a realm stuffed with natural resources cannily exploited. Trade with the Byzantines was steady and heavy, bringing back not just their goods but their arts and ideas. The Russian upper classes, more capitalists than noblemen, were literate, *au courant* with events abroad as well as at home; they lived in houses equipped with stoves and window glass; they ate with gold and silver spoons, off plates set on sumptuous tablecloths, the meals including delicacies like oranges, lemons, and sugar; dogs, never allowed indoors, had shelters of their own, and customarily a Hungarian groom to care for them and the horses; Kiev in particular was a cosmopolitan home for a dozen different nationalities; the monarchy was not despotic, rather the system granted so much freedom that popular assemblies, in Novgorod especially, often turned into brawls—

The point was that Oleg could place himself exactly in space and time: the eastward bend of the Dnieper, early June, 1050 A.D.

Uldin, vaguer, had spoken of recently taking over the land of the East Goths, after having first crushed the Alans, and of greedy speculations about the Roman Empire to the west. From his dippings into history (thank fortune for a good memory!) Reid could delimit the Hun's scene of departure: the Ukraine, one or two hundred miles from the Crimea in a more or less northwesterly direction; time, the later fourth century A.D.

Erissa posed the trickiest problem, for all her eager cooperation. The name of the island whence she had been seized, Malath, was that bestowed by its largely Keftiu inhabitants. The English equivalent did not automatically come to Reid, any more than he would have known Christiana and Oslo were identical if he had not been so informed.

He set aside the riddle of her former home, Atlantis. A continent that sank? Pure myth; geological impossibility, in any period less than millions of years. And yet the name as used by her bore such a freight of the same meaning, the fair and happy realm which the sea took back unto itself, that it had come through the helmet as more than a label. . . . Well, she said her Atlantis was gone. Where had she lived afterward? Might a clue be found in what that other folk whose language she also knew called the place?

"Rodhos," she told him, and all at once he understood. A few queries about its exact location *vis-à-vis* the mainland clinched the matter. Rhodes.

He shut his eyes and visualized, again, a terrestrial globe. It was reasonable to assume the space-time vehicle had followed the most nearly direct geographical course it could. The assumption was strengthened by the fact that Hawaii, the ship's position in the North Pacific, the bend of the Dnieper, the southern Ukraine, and Rhodes did lie approximately on a great circle.

Okay, Reid thought in rising, tingling excitement. Extrapolate. What's the next shore you hit?

Western Egypt or eastern Libya. A seacoast desert, if I remember aright.

He opened his eyes. Erissa's hazel gaze was waiting for him. Briefly, he almost drowned in it. He yanked himself back from beauty and said, "I think I have reasoned out where we are."

"Oh, Duncan!" She rose to her knees and hugged him. Tired, thirsty, hungry, in mortal trouble, he felt her breasts press, her lips touch.

Oleg coughed. Erissa let Reid go. The American sought to explain. It took a minute, because the woman called Egypt "Khem," which she said was the native as well as Keftiu name. When she grasped his intent, a little of the happiness went out of her. "Yes, the Achaeans say 'Aigyptos.' Does so scant a recollection of my poor folk remain in your world?"

"Egypt." Oleg tugged his beard. "That fits, gauging by what I've heard from sailors who ply the route. Myself, I never got further than Jerusalem." He cocked a glance at the improvised canopy and heaven above. "I was on pilgrimage," he reminded the saints. "The Saracens made endless fuss and inconvenience. I brought back a flask of Jordan water and gave it to the Sophia Cathedral that *Knyaz* Yaroslav the Wise built in Kiev."

Erissa brightened. "We have no bad chance of rescue. Ships go to and from Egypt throughout the summer." Distress descended anew upon her. She winced at a tormenting recollection. "The crew might take us only to sell for slaves, though."

Reid patted her knee. "I have a trick or two that should discourage them," he said more confidently than he felt, just to see her glow.

Wait a bit, flashed within him. If she knows anything about contemporary Egypt, maybe that'll give me a date. Not that I'm really up on Pharaonic chronology—this period's got to be Pharaonic—but . . .

Irrelevantly, his intellect drew a graph of the futurian machine's path, distance covered versus time. Assuming Sahir's era was some centuries beyond the American's, and Erissa's one or a few thousand years before Christ, you got a diagram resembling half a hysteresis curve. Might that be significant, might it help explain the "inertia" effect? Never mind, never mind.

"Hee-yah!" The shout brought their heads out from under the cloths. Uldin sat his horse atop the bluff which fronted on the beach. The gestures of his saber were violent. They hurried from the water, scrambled into their garments and up the rough hot slope.

The Hun was furious. He spat at their feet. "Lolling about like hogs! Do you claim you're men, you two?"

Oleg hefted his ax, Erissa her knife. Reid swallowed. He thought: I'm not the one to respond. I'm the shy guy, the stutterer, the citizen who does nothing in politics except vote, the husband who quietly walks away when an argument brews with his wife—

Somehow he looked up into the seamed features and said: "Better we keep our health and wits than rush about like beetles, Uldin. I spent the time getting facts. Now we know where we are and what we can await."

The Hun's face went blank. After a moment he replied: "You did not say you are a shaman, Duncan, nor do I believe you are. But you may have more wisdom than I thought. Let's not quarrel, let's make ready. I saw men from afar, headed this way. They're on foot, a scrawny and tattered lot, but they're armed and I didn't like the look of them. If a herdboy went to their camp this dawn and told how last night he'd seen a treasure that shone and a mere four to guard it, they'd come here."

"Umph," Oleg said. "When will they arrive?"

"They could make it by high noon. But my guess is they'll rest during the heat of the day. Toward evening, then."

"Good. I needn't don that oven of a byrnie at once. Should we flee?"

Reid shook his head. "The odds are against our getting far," he said. "We might shake off pursuit, but the desert will kill us. Let's stay where we are and think how we can bargain with the natives."

"Bargaining goes hard when your throat's cut," Uldin laughed. "Pack your gear. If we wade the first part of the way, it'll break our trail."

"You suppose they can't be reasoned with," Reid argued.

Oleg and Uldin peered at him. "Why, of course they can't," the Russian said. "They're wasteland dwellers."

"Can't we at least overawe them? I'd rather stay here and try what can be done than stagger off to die in three or four miserable days."

Uldin slapped his thigh, a pistol crack. "Get moving!" he ordered.

"No," Reid answered.

Erissa took his arm. "You two go if you are afraid," she said scornfully. "We stay."

Oleg scratched his shaggy chest. "Well," he mumbled. "Well . . . me too. You may be right."

Uldin gave them a freezing glare. They stood firm beneath his saddle. "You leave me no choice," he snapped. "What's your plan?"

Put up or shut up, Reid thought, and he wondered if this was how leaders were made. "I'll work on a show that may impress them," he said. "We have the vehicle itself—and, for instance—" He demonstrated his pipe lighter. The spurt of flame drew exclamations. "We'll want defenses, of course, in case we do have to fight. You, Uldin, Oleg, take charge of that. I should imagine that between you—a mounted bowman, an ironclad warrior— you'll make a pack of starvelings wary about attacking. Erissa, you and I will gather sticks for a signal fire, in case a ship comes by."

—She said to him when they were working alone: "I wonder more and more if this is wise, Duncan. A captain might not dare stand in. He might take our beacon for a lure. Or if he does land, he might well see us as prey, to be robbed and enslaved. Maybe we should trust in the Goddess and our ability to make the desert folk guide us to Egypt. The sea lanes grow ever more perilous and cruel, when the strong hand of the Minos is no longer lifted against piracy."

"Minos!" he cried, jarred; and the knowledge of where and when he was stood blindingly before him.

He started to ask her out—the Keftiu, yes, the people of Keft, a large island in the Midworld Sea between Egypt and those lands the Achaeans had overrun—Crete!—yes, the second language she knew was Achaean, everybody with foreign connections must master it, now that those barbarians were swarming into the Aegean Sea and too arrogant to learn the speech once spoken in stately Knossos and on lost Atlantis—

*Achaean* ran through Reid. He had no more Greek than the average educated twentieth-century American, but that was enough to open for him the identity of the tongue he had learned. He saw past the patterns of an alphabet which hadn't evolved yet, to the language itself, and knew that Achaean was an ancestor of Hellenic.

And that was where the name Atlantis came from. "Land of the Pillar" translated into *Gaia Atlantis*.

"Sail ho!" Oleg bellowed.

The ship was large for its milieu, a ninety-footer. When there was no fair wind, it put out fifty oars. The hull, black with pitch, was wide amidships (Erissa said this was a merchantman, not a slender warcraft), rounded in the stern, rising sheer from a cutwater in the bows. Stem and stern alike were decked over, protected by wicker bulwarks and ornamented with carved and colored posts in the forms of a horsehead and a fishtail. Two huge painted eyes stared forward. Under the rowing benches that stretched between the sides, planks were laid so that men need not clamber across the cargo stowed in the bottom. At present the mast was down; it, the yard, and the sail were lashed in the crotches of two Y-shaped racks fore and aft. Keel barely aground in the shallows, the vessel waited.

Most of its crew stayed aboard, alert. Sun glared off bronze spearheads. Otherwise metal was scarce. The squarish shields had only rivets securing several plies of boiled cowhide to wooden frames. The common sailor made do with body protection of leather over a tunic like Erissa's, or with none.

Diores, the captain, and the seven young men who accompanied him ashore were a gorgeous exception. They could afford the best; shortage of copper and tin was the economic foundation of the military aristocracy which ruled most of the Bronze Age world. In high-plumed helmets, ornate breastplates, brass facings on shields and on the leather strips that dangled past their kilts, greaves on shins, leaf-shaped swords in gold-ornamented scabbards, cloaks dyed in reds and blues and saffrons, they might have walked straight out of the *Iliad*.

They'll walk straight into it, Reid thought eerily. Asking, he had learned Troy was a strong and prosperous city-state; but here before him stood the Achaeans—Danaans, Argives, Hellenes—the forebears of Agamemnon and Odysseus.

They were tall, fair-complexioned, long-skulled men, their own progenitors come down from the North not very many generations back; brown hair was ordinary among them, yellow and red not rare. They wore it shoulder-length, and those who could raise a beard and mustache—the percentage of youths was high—favored a kind of Vandyke style. They carried themselves with the almost unconscious haughtiness of warriors born.

"Well, now," Diores said. "Strange. Strange in truth, 'tis."

The castaways had decided not to complicate an already incredible story with a time travel element that none but the American came anywhere near comprehending anyway. It was more than sufficient that they had been carried here from their respective homelands by the glowing chariot of a wizard who died before he could get beyond demonstrating his magical language teacher. Diores had ordered the body uncovered, and properly buried after his inspection.

He clicked his tongue. "Zeus thunder me, what a weird yarn!" He put a habitual drawl into the generally rapid-fire Attic dialect. "I don't know as how I ought to take you aboard. I honestly don't. You could be under the wrath of a god."

"But—but—" Reid waved helplessly at the *mentatór* set. "We'll give that to your king."

Diores squinted. He was smaller and darker than most of his followers, grizzled, but tough, quick-moving, eyes winter-gray in the seamed sharp countenance. "Well, now, don't get me wrong," he said. "I'd like to. By Aphrodite's tits, I'd like to. You particular, sir—" he nodded at Oleg—"clad in the foreign metal iron. We hear rumors they've learned how to work it in Hittite lands but the Great King's keeping that secret for himself. Might you know—? Oh, we could spin many a fine yarn. But what's the use if Poseidon whelms us? And he has a touchy temper, Poseidon does, this time of year; the equinoctial storms'll soon be along." His calculating gaze strayed to Uldin, who had remained mounted. "And you, sir, that ride your horse 'stead of coming behind in a chariot, I'd give a fat ox to know what the idea is. Won't you fall off in battle? And you want to take the beast aboard!"

"I'll not be parted from him," Uldin snapped.

"Horses are sacred to Poseidon, aren't they?" Reid put in quickly.

"Yes, true, true, but the practical problems . . . we already have a brace of sheep and our land-finding doves. And some days' faring to reach home, you know. And I'll tell you confidential, this hasn't been a plain trading trip. Not quite. Oh, we laid to at Avaris and the men bartered and enjoyed the inns and stews, right, right. But a few of us traveled upriver to Memphis, the capital, you know, bearing a word from my prince, and now I've a word to take back to him. Can't risk losing that, can I, me who's served the royal family man and boy since before the prince was born?"

"Will you keep us here sweltering the whole day, till the tribesmen arrive?" Uldin yelled.

"Calm down," Oleg told him. He studied Diores, his mien as pawky as the Achaean's. "It's true we'll cause you extra trouble, Captain," he murmured. "I'm sorry for that. But might you accept—a gift between gentlemen, naturally, a slight repayment for your noble generosity when you broached yon water cask for us—would you allow me to show you, as well as your king, that we're not beggars?"

He had dipped into his purse while he talked. The gold coins flashed for half a second before Diores' deft fingers closed on them.

"Plain to see, you're folk of good breeding," the Achaean said blandly, "and that alone obliges me to help you in any way I can. Do come aboard. Do. The horse—sir, if you'll agree to sacrifice your horse here on this shore for a safe voyage, you can have your pick out of my own herd when we arrive. That I swear."

Uldin muttered but gave in. Diores made a welcoming gesture at his ship.

"Rhodes first," Erissa said. Ecstasy flooded from her. "Duncan, Duncan, you'll see our son!"

Reid's stupefaction and her joy were cut off by Diores: "I'm afraid not. I *am* on a mission for Prince Theseus, and can't go out of my way. The only reason we came this far west after leaving the Nile Delta was—"

"Fear of the pirates in the Aegean islands," she said bitterly.

"What? Pirates? Has the sun addled your wits? No disrespect, m' lady. I know how high womenfolk rank among the Cretans, and you must have been a sacred bull dancer when young, right? Nothing else would explain that carriage of yours. Ah, yes. But as for pirates, no, never; d'you think we're in Tyrrhenian waters? It's simply that, with the wind as is, I gauge our best course is around the west end of Crete and then slide along past the Peloponnesus to Athens. You can take passage thence for Rhodes, next spring at latest."

In her disappointment she was not mollified. "You speak as if the Minos and his navy still kept the peace of the sea for honest folk." Venom edged her voice.

"I do believe you should go aboard and rest, my lady, out of the sun." Diores' geniality stayed unbroken. "Last time I called at Knossos, and that was outbound on this trip to leave off some cargo, hardly a month back, the Minos sat in the Labyrinth and his customs officers were battening on his tithe same as always."

She whitened.

"Worse luck," growled a subordinate officer. "How long, Father Zeus, must we bear his yoke?" His friends looked equally angered.

# SEVEN

At first shipboard was paradise. Reid, stunned by an avalanche of experiences and impressions like none he had imagined—for no historical novelist could give him the total *reality*—needed day and night and part of the day that followed to see that shipboard was, in fact, only the absence of hell.

Fed (salt beef, leeks, coarse black bread, mixed wine and water), cooled by a breeze that ruffled his hair, beneath a soft clear sky, amidst the sun's million sparks flung off a thousand shades of deep, moving, snowy-foamed blue: he sat by a rail and remembered Homer's line about the multitudinous laughter of the waves. They were smaller than on the ocean, friskier, very close to him as they passed beneath the low gunwale. He could see each ripple and swirl; he marveled anew at how intricate, ever-changing a piece of art was a wave.

The ship plowed forward, a bone in her teeth and wake whirling aft. The decks rocked in a long rhythm, timbers creaked, stays hummed, sometimes a sheet would go *snap* and the sail thutter to a change of wind or sea. The air, mild and lively, was rich with odors of sun-baked pitch, ozone, saltiness. On the poop the quartermasters—a craft this size had both port and starboard steering oars—stood watch like young gods.

The rest of the crew sat at ease when they were not sprawled under the thwarts for a nap (nude, using the tunic for a pillow, but generally rolled in a sheepskin blanket). Quarters were cramped. However, no trip involved more than a few days continuously afloat; as a rule, vessels hugged the coasts and their crews camped ashore every night.

The men's eyes kept straying toward the passengers, half

curious, half fearful. Who knew what these strangers were? It took a while before any save Diores and his noblemen ventured to say any word beyond a muttered greeting. The sailors talked low-toned among each other, they fiddled at small chores, they made furtive signs which Reid had seen while he traveled about in Mediterranean parts on leave from the Army, thousands of years from now.

No matter. They'd get over their shyness when nothing terrible happened. And he was bound for Athens!

Not the Athens he'd loved, he reminded himself. The temples on the Acropolis, the Tower of the Winds, the columns of Olympian Zeus—tiny friendly cafés, their *dolmades* and *tourko* and *ouzo*, smart shops, insane taxi drivers, old women in black, vendors of hard-roasted corn on the cob, cheerful men who all seem to have cousins in Brooklyn—forget them, because you dare not remember. Forget, too, Aristotle, Pericles, Aeschylus, the victory at Marathon, the siege of Troy, Homer himself. None of it exists, unless perhaps a few tribal chants have lines that will someday be preserved in an epic and thus endure after their makers are millennial dust. Everything else is a ghost, no, less than a ghost, a vision, a fading dream.

You're bound for the Athens of Prince Theseus.

That much will last to your day. You'll be thrilled in your boyhood to read how a hero named Theseus slew the gruesome Minotaur—

A shadow fell across him.

—the Minotaur which Erissa served.

She joined him, ignoring the crewmen who, crowded back to leave them alone on this bench, kept looking and looking. A borrowed cloak was fastened, not over the shoulders of her tunic but about her waist to form a skirt.

"Why?" Reid asked, pointing at the garment.

She shrugged. "Best I muffle myself like an Achaean woman." The Keftiu words fell flatly out of her mouth. She stared at the horizon.

"Isn't this wonderful?" he said, trying clumsily to hearten

her. "I can understand why Aphrodite was born from the sea foam."

"What?" Her eyes, turned the hue of dull jade, swung to him. "What do you speak of?"

"Why, why don't the Achaeans," he stammered, "don't they believe the goddess of . . . love . . . rose from the sea off Cyprus?"

She sneered. "Aphrodite, cow-teated, barrel-buttocked, the bitch forever in heat?"

Reid cast an alarmed glance past her. Probably quite a few of those men had a working knowledge of Cretan. Nobody seemed to have heard, though, through the singing air.

"The Goddess, yes, in Her form of Britomartis the Maiden, She arose thus," Erissa said.

He thought: I suppose the Achaeans kept—will keep—the beautiful myth, giving it to what's now a primitive fertility figure . . . after Crete has been overthrown.

Erissa's fist smote the rail. "The sea is Hers—and ours!" she cried. "What spell made you forget, Duncan?"

"I tell you, I'm a mortal man, more lost than you are," he said desperately. "I'm trying to find out what's happened to us. You've gone backward in time yourself, and—"

"Hush." Self-controlled again, she laid a hand on his arm and whispered: "Not here. Later, as soon as may be, but not here. That Diores isn't the yokel he pretends. He watches, listens, probes. And he is the enemy."

Traffic was thinning out as stormy autumn approached, but they spoke two other ships on their first afternoon. One, rowing into the wind, was a Keftiu-owned freighter, though its crew seemed to be drawn from the whole eastern Mediterranean, bound from Pylos with hides which ought to fetch a goodly amount of timber in Lebanon. The skipper expected to take the wood on to Egypt and swap it for glassware before returning to his home port on Naxos for a season's ease. Diores explained that such runs had become profitable again since Pharaoh

Amenhotep pacified his Syrian province. The other and larger vessel boomed straight toward Avaris, carrying British tin. Its men were still more mixed, including some who, glimpsed across unrestful scores of yards, appeared to be North European recruits. The world today was astonishingly more cosmopolitan than it would be later on in history.

And once, miles off, Reid glimpsed the reason for that. A lean galley quartered the horizon. Several of Diores' people drew knives at it or made obscene gestures. "What's yonder craft?" Oleg inquired.

"A Cretan warship," Diores replied. "On patrol."

"For distressed mariners," Erissa said, "and against pirates and barbarians."

"Against those who'd be free," an Achaean boy declared hotly.

"No squabbles," Diores commanded. The boy slouched aft. Erissa clenched her lips and spoke no more.

Soon after dark the breeze died and the vessel lay hove to under magnificent stars. Gazing at them before he slept, Reid recalled that they too were not eternal. "Tell me," he asked Erissa, "what constellation heads your Zodiac?"

"The Bull, of course, Asterion's Bull, when he awakens from death in the reborn spring." Her voice, which had started sharp, ended in reverence. Through the wan light he saw her kiss her amulet and trace a sign amidst shadow, a cross, the sun's emblem.

Precession of the equinoxes, he thought. I've come back two twelfths of twenty-six thousand years. Well, that isn't so exact. He shivered, though the night was not especially cold, and crept under a thwart to huddle in the sheepskin Diores had lent him.

At dawn they took down the mast, broke out the oars, and spider-walked to the coxswain's chant—*"Rhypapai! Rhypapai!"*—creaking and splashing across a sea which shimmered pale blue at first, later sapphire above indigo. Oleg said he wanted exercise and settled down at an oar for two turns in a stretch.

That cracked the men's reserve. When the breeze lifted (not as favorable as yesterday's, but Reid was surprised to learn how close this awkward-looking square rig could point) they gathered about the Russian, who sat dangling his legs off the foredeck. They gave him undiluted wine and bestormed him with questions.

"Where you from, stranger?—What's it like?—Where've you been?—What kinds of ship they use in your country?—That armor you were wearing, those weapons, are they really iron?—Iron's no good, too brittle, even when you can get it out of its ore, which I've heard is mucking near impossible. What's the trick?—Hai, how're your women?—Your wine? D'you drink beer like Egyptians?" Teeth flashed in brown countenances, bodies shifted around in a dance of muscles, laughter and chatter pealed across the blueness.

Could these frank, merry boys, these far-faring men with skillful hands, be the savages Erissa claimed they were?

She sat on a bench well aft, brooding. Uldin shared it. They didn't speak. The Hun had uttered hardly a sound after the hour yesterday when he must lean overside while the Achaeans guffawed at his back. He'd gotten over the sickness, but stayed sullen at the loss of face. Or did he crouch alone behind his mask in a wretchedness of terror? This endless water where no horse could move!

Diores lounged on the deck beside Oleg, picking his teeth and saying little. Reid sat nervously nearby, against the bulwark, embracing knees under chin, hoping the Russian wouldn't make some gaffe, as hard as he was drinking. He was no fool, but after everything which had lately happened to him the temptation to lower his guard and relax must be considerable.

"I'm a man of the Rus, if that's what you mean." Oleg drained his beaker and passed it down for more. His yellow locks fluttered from the headband, his eyes twinkled happily in the red cherubic visage, he scratched beneath his shirt and belched. "Don't know 'bout the rest. S'pose I lay out the land for you, and you tell me what you rec'nize. That way we'll get the names straight."

They settled back to listen. He swigged from the refilled cup and rumbled:

"I'll start far north. You might like to hear 'bout that. Woods, mile after mile of woods. Farms too, of course, but you could wander in the woods your whole life. I almost did when I was a sprat. My father was a merchant, wiped out when first the Poles took Novgorod, then Yaroslav took it back, then the long war 'tween Yaroslav and his brother stopped our trade south. We went into those woods, took up hunting and trapping. I learned how to get about there, I can tell you. The Finns have, uh, wooden shoes for walking on snow. They're wizards. Told me how to sing up a good wind, though it doesn't always work for me and, uh, naturally a Christian shouldn't." They registered puzzlement, since to them he had just said that he was an anointed one; but evidently they decided he must be an initiate of some mystery cult.

"We came back at last, started over in better times, and I've not done badly. Learned another lesson from those early days, too." Oleg chuckled, drank, and wagged his forefinger. "Trade stopped again, or nearly so, for a couple years after our war with Constantinople. I spent that time in Norway. The king's a good friend to the Rus; served a while under Yaroslav, in fact; married a daughter of his. I got together many a load of furs in that country. First time I returned to Constantinople, believe you me, I made a killing."

"You were speaking of your homeland," a man called.

"Ah. So I was. Novgorod. Would you believe, well inland as 'tis, Novgorod's a seaport? Row from Gulf of Finland, up the Neva, 'cross Lake Ladoga, up the Volkhov to Lake Ilmen, and there you are. 'Course, you can't go on. You've got to ride overland, make rendezvous on the Dnieper, first. But then it's water the whole way, 'cept for the rapids. Kiev's grown big and fat off that waterway, I can tell you. But me, I stay a Novgorod boy, where the furs and amber are handier to come by. And so at last you reach the Black Sea, and turn south along the coast to Constantinople, and *there's* a city, lads, there you have the queen o' the world."

"Hold on," Diores said slowly. "What you call the Black Sea, does it lead through two straits, a small sea between them, to these waters?"

Oleg nodded vigorously. "You have it hooked. Constantinople's at the inner end of the northern channel."

"But there's no city there," a crewman protested.

"Oh, you'd not have heard, I suppose," Oleg said loftily.

"Zeus thunder me, I have!" Diores rapped, all at once become stern. Silence took over, except for thrum and gurgle and the pitiful bleat of the two sheep penned beneath this deck. "I've plied these lanes aplenty, you," Diores said. "Once as far as Colchis under the Caucasus. Nor am I the only Achaean who has."

"You mean you dare those currents in a cockleshell like this?" Oleg exclaimed. "Why, I could almos' put my fist through the side."

"A guest oughtn't to tell lies," Diores said.

"Wait," Reid began, reaching to touch him.

Oleg shook his head. "Sorry. Too much wine." He stared into his cup. "I forgot. We've come backward through time. Constantinople's not been built yet, I s'pose. It will be, though, it will be. I've been there. I know." He tossed the wine off and the cup down into a sailor's lap.

Diores stayed unmoving. His face might have been a block of driftwood. The listeners below stirred and buzzed. Hands dropped toward bronze knives; fingers traced signs.

"Oleg," Reid said. "No more."

"Why not?" the Russian mumbled. "Truth, isn' it? Let's go in business as prophets."

"No more," Reid repeated. "I've told you where *I* am from. Heed me."

Oleg bit his lip. Reid turned to Diores. Above the unease that crawled inside him and made his skin prickle, the American donned an apologetic grin. "I should have warned you, Captain," he said. "My comrade's given to tall tales. And of course what really happened would confuse anybody."

"I think we'd better hold off on this kind of talk," Diores suggested. "Till we're in the palace in Athens. Right?"

# EIGHT

THE ATMOSPHERE did not turn unfriendly. The sailors obviously dismissed the incomprehensible remarks about time travel, setting that down to a misunderstanding quite natural when the speaker was from parts as remote as Oleg became careful to put his Russia and Byzantine Empire. It helped that, far from being accursed, this passage enjoyed unusually fair winds. Reid wasn't sure how much was believed of what the Novgorodian related—and the Hun, after he came out of his shell; but everybody liked a good yarn. For their part, the crew were glad of fresh ears for their own stories: trading voyages where the Minoan navy kept watch, plundering and slave raiding elsewhere; hunting on the mainland, deer, bear, pig, the aurochs and lion that still roamed Europe; clashes with wild mountaineers or with other Achaean statelets; brawls, binges, lickerish recollections of harbortown hetaerae and temples in Asia where a maiden must take the first man who would have her before she could marry; tales, solemnly sworn to, of gods and ghosts and monsters. . . .

Reid avoided saying much about his milieu and concentrated on learning about this. The Achaeans were a race of husbandmen, he was told. The very kings plowed their own fields and did their own carpentry. The poorest yeoman had his jealously guarded rights. Among the turbulent nobles (those men wealthy enough to own the full panoply of bronze war-gear that made a common soldier easy meat for them) the king (the sachem, Reid thought) was no more than *primus inter pares*. Women did not have the complete equality of their Keftiu sisters, which

Diores scoffed at as hen-predominance; but neither did they suffer the purdah of Classical Greece; a matron was honored in her household.

Only for a few generations, and thus far only in a few of their countries, had the Achaeans taken to the sea in any numbers. Diores was one of the rare skippers among them who would boldly strike straight across a days-wide stretch of open water, which the Keftiu routinely did. But his folk were superb stockbreeders and charioteers; not a man of them but wasn't a fanatical expert on horseflesh, and their note-comparing and arguing with Uldin rattled on for hours at a time.

They stood unshakable by their families, their chieftains, and their pledged word. A man was expected to be as hospitable and open-handed as his means allowed. He kept himself clean, well groomed, and in trim; he knew the lore and laws; he appreciated quality in an artisan, a dancer, a bard; he looked misfortune and death squarely in the eyes.

Against this, Reid could place a pride that might at any instant bring on a fit of the sulks or of murderousness; a bloodthirsty delight in battle; an absolute lack of feeling for anyone considered inferior—and if you were not a freeborn Achaean or a pretty damn powerful foreigner, you were inferior; a quarrelsomeness that kept the people divided into contending micro-kingdoms which often split further in civil war.

"There's a reason the Cretans lord it over us," Diores remarked, standing in the bows beside Reid while he observed the flight of a released dove. "Could be the top reason. We can't pull together. Not that the Labyrinth ever gives us a chance to. The big mainland cities, Mycenae, Tiryns, that gaggle, they've sold out. Cretan wares, Cretan manners, Cretan rites, Cretan this and that till a man could puke. How I wish they'd go the whole road and put themselves straight under the Minos! But no, he's too smart, that'n. He keeps their bootlicker kings, who can sit at council with ours, plot and bribe and turn true Achaean against Achaean. And when somebody plans a break for freedom, the way my King Aegeus did, be sure a spy from Mycenae or Tiryns will find out and squirm off to squeal it in Knossos."

"And then?" Reid asked.

"Why, then the Minos whistles up his navy and blockades every port and grabs the ships of every vassal and—argh!—'ally' who won't send men to help. So they help him. And that's why next year seven more boys and seven more girls will fare from Athens to the Minotaur."

Diores broke off, shaded his eyes, peered ahead for a while, until he said in a casual tone: "There she be. Now you can begin to see what the bird saw. Can you make out that little blur on the world-edge? A peak on Crete. Got to be, I swear by Aphrodite's belly."

They rounded the great island before sundown. Cliffs stood white. Behind, the country lifted steep and green. Vessels crossed the waters as thickly as gulls crossed the sky. Erissa stood by the rail, looking. She had made no show of unhappiness these past days. She had merely spoken no more than was needful, and otherwise sat alone with her thoughts. Reid sought her.

Her face did not turn toward him. He wondered what fears and longings dwelt behind that clear profile. As if reading his mind, she said low, "Don't fret yourself about me, Duncan. The years have taught me how to wait."

Next eventide the Peloponnesus rose rugged from violet waves. The open hills, speckled with villages, and the water traffic that Reid remembered were not here. Forest lay deeply green; loneliness filled sea and sky, a quiet in which the *chunk* and splash of oars sounded too noisy and the coxswain softened his chant. The air was cool. A pair of cranes, high aloft, caught the light golden on their wings.

Diores indicated the island of Kythera a few miles offshore. It resembled a piece of the mainland. "Two days left to the Piraeus, maybe less," he said. "But we'll stop here the night, give a thank-offering for an easy voyage, stretch our legs and sleep where we've got room to turn around in."

The beach in a little bay bore signs of use: fire-blackened

circles of rock, bits of rope and other inoffensive refuse, a beehive-shaped stone tomb opposite a crude wooden god whose most conspicuous feature was the phallus, a trail winding inward under the trees toward what Diores said was a spring. But tonight his ship had the site to itself. The sailors grounded the hull, put a boulder anchor astern and took a hawser along when they waded ashore.

Uldin reeled on his feet. "This place is haunted!" he roared, drew his saber and glared about him. "The land wobbles!"

"It'll stop," Oleg grinned. "Here's a good medicine for that." He ran to join the men who were uncramping themselves by footraces, wrestling matches, leapfrogging, and war whoops. Diores let them go on for half an hour before he called them to make camp, gather wood and start a fire.

Erissa had sought the tomb. Leaving the cloak around her lower body, she pulled off her tunic; bare-breasted, she knelt, clutched her amulet and bent her loose-tressed head in prayer. Diores looked uneasy. "I wish I'd halted her," he muttered to Reid. "Would've, if I'd noticed in time."

"What's she doing?"

"Asking for an oracle dream, I suppose. I wanted to do that. He's said to be uncommon powerful, the man buried here. Now I can't; he might not like it twice in the same evening. And I'd have given him part of the sacrifice, too." Diores tugged his beard, scowling. "I wonder what vow she's making in its place. That's no ordinary she-Cretan, Duncan, mate; not even an ordinary sister of the bull dance. There's something peculiar about her. I'd give her a wide berth if I was you."

Erissa resumed her tunic and stood aside. She seemed to have gained a measure of inward calm. Reid didn't venture to address her. He was finding out how alien her world was to him.

Night had fallen before the campfire coals were ready to roast the sheep which had been brought from Egypt for this landing. The sacrifice was brief but impressive: tall men standing ranked in leaping red light and wavering shadow, weapons lifted in salute to Hermes the Wayfarer; Diores' chanted invocation; his solemn slaughter of the animals, cutting out of the thighbones, wrapping them in fat, casting them in the fire; deep-voiced "Xareis! Xareis! Xareis!" rising like the smoke toward the stars; clangor of swords beaten on helmets and brass-faced shields.

Oleg crossed himself. Uldin nicked his thumb and squeezed some blood into the flames. Reid couldn't see Erissa in the dark.

She shared the meal that followed. It was a light-hearted gorge. The wineskins passed freely. Afterward a warrior stood, plucked a lyre and chanted a lay—

"—*Raging arose Hippothous, far-famed slayer of hillmen,*
*He who had burned their camps and left their men for the vultures,*
*Bearing away the women and gold and head of Lord Skedyon.*
*Loud in his hand twanged the bow, and eager the arrow went leaping—*"

—while his comrades stamped out a dance on the sand.

When they sat down, Uldin rose. "I will sing you a song," he offered.

"Then me," Oleg said. "A song of a wanderer far from his home, his dear ones, his Mother Novgorod." He dabbed at his eyes and hiccoughed.

"Mine is of the steppe," Uldin said, "the grassland where poppies flare like blood in springtime and the foals stand on unsure new legs, their muzzles softer than a girl baby's cheek, and dream of the day when they shall gallop untiring to the roots of the rainbow."

He lifted his head. The words were in his own language, but the melody and his voice astonishingly sweet.

Reid had planted himself well back from the group around the fire, to observe. Abruptly he felt his sleeve plucked. Turning, he made out Erissa's vague form. His heart skipped a beat. He rose, quietly as possible, and slipped after her, around the circle of light to the trail.

It was dark under the trees. They groped their way hand in hand. After some minutes' uphill stumbling, they came out in the open.

Surrounded on three sides by forest, a meadow sloped down to the shore. The moon was aloft, waning toward the half. Reid had often admired it at sea before going to sleep; but this was sorcery. Full over an empty ocean, it had not cast the glade it did on these waters of Erissa's Goddess, which lay so still that stars and a lamp-white planet were mirrored in their night. Grass and boulders were starred also, with dewdrops. The air here was warmer than at the strand, as if the woods breathed out the day they had hoarded. Their odor was of damp mould, leaves, pungencies. An owl hooted gently. The spring rilled between mossy stones.

Erissa sighed. "I hoped for this," she said low: "a place that must be holy with Her nearness, where we can talk."

He had dreaded that. But now, the moment come, he knew her sense of fate, neither sad nor glad, a strong resignation he had never thought might be.

She spread her cloak. They sat down, facing the water. Her fingers stroked the beard growing on him. He saw by moonlight how tender was her smile. "You come daily closer to the Duncan I knew," she murmured.

"Tell me what happened," he said as quietly.

She shook her head. "I am not sure. I recall very little from the end, shards, fading mists, here a hand that consoled me, there a word spoken—and the witch, the witch who made me sleep and forget. . . ." She sighed again. "A mercy, perhaps, to judge from what horrors remain to me. I've often wished the same veil drawn over what came afterward."

She gripped his hand, painfully hard. "We in the boat—Dagonas and I—thought to make for the eastern islands, find refuge in one of the Keftiu colonies," she said. "But we could not see sun or sky through those lightning-riven clouds, through the ashen rain; and the waters were torn, crazed by the hurt that had come to them; and then a wind sprang up, driving us helpless before its howling. We could just keep afloat. When at last it grew calmer, we spied a ship. But they were Trojans aboard, bound home after the blackness terrified them from the voyage they had embarked on. They made us captive; and when we got there, we went for slaves."

She drew breath. No matter what she had gained from the sight of Crete or from the oracular hero, these were deep wounds she was breaking open afresh. Reid's calm was shaken too. Automatically, he drew forth pipe and tobacco.

The distraction might have been ordained by the Goddess' infant Son in prankish kindliness, as Erissa suggested with an unsteady small laugh. By the time he had explained what he was about, she could speak almost detachedly. He comforted himself with the love-bite of smoke and listened, his fingers enfolding hers:

"My purchaser was called Mydon. He was of Achaean blood—they've bought and bullied their way into the Troad too, did you know?—but not the worst of masters, really. And Dagonas was there. He'd showed himself off, courting Mydon, to be taken along with me, and got to be a clerk for him. Thus we ended in the same household. I do remember how you, Duncan, gave me into Dagonas' care when we parted. And still you deny you're a god?

"When Deukalion was born—your son; I know with all my blood he must be yours—I named him thus because it sounded close to your name, and because I swore he likewise would become the father of nations—I couldn't let him be raised a slave. I bided my time for a second year, watching, planning, preparing. Dagonas grew patient also, after I showed him how there must be a fate in this. When at last we slipped away, Deukalion in my arms, I meant to leave Mydon's daughter out of me strangled, my farewell gift to him. But she was so tiny in her crib, I couldn't. I hope he has let her have some happiness.

"We took the boat we'd hidden and provisioned, and set off. Our aim was to creep south to the Dodecanese Keftiu. Again the wind was foul, though, driving us north till we stranded on the shores of Thrace. There we found refuge among the wild hillfolk and abode for several years. At first we were welcome because we made gifts of things we'd stolen from Troy. Later Dagonas became an important man because he's clever and knows many Keftiu arts. For my part, though I was only a lay sister on Atlantis, not a priestess, I taught them things about the worship of the Goddess and Asterion that pleased them. In return, they took me into their guild of witches. There, besides magic, I gained healing craft unknown in Greece or the islands— herbs, treatments, the casting of the Sleep—and these have since given me stature where I live. So it was no ill-willing god who blew us to Thrace. It must have been the destiny you laid on me.

"In the end, having gained some wealth, we could buy passage from a Rhodian trader. At his home port we found distant kin-folk of mine, who helped us start anew. At last we were well off.

"But I am no longer the girl you loved, Duncan."

A silence lingered. The water sang, the owl crossed beneath the moon on phantom wings. Reid cradled his warm pipe and Erissa's clasping hand.

"Nor am I the god you remember," he said at length. "I never was."

"Maybe a god used you and has since gone away. You're not less dear for that."

He put the pipe down, twisted about to confront her—how luminous those eyes!—and said gravely, "You must try to understand. We've all come back into the past. You too. At this moment, I feel sure, the girl who was you is alive on an Atlantis that has not foundered."

"That *will* not." Her voice rang. "This is why we were sent here, Duncan: that we, forewarned, may save our people."

He couldn't reply.

The tone softened: "But how I have longed for you, how I have dreamed. Am I grown too old, my darling?"

It was as if someone else answered. "No. You never will."

He himself thought: Yes, O Christ, an act of kindness if

nothing else. No, now come off that. You've had a couple of romps Pam hasn't needed to be told about, and Christ, Pam won't be born for three or four thousand years, and Erissa is here and beautiful. . . . But it was not himself thinking after all; it was the stranger, the outcast from an unreal tomorrow. Himself was the one who had spoken aloud.

Weeping and laughing, Erissa took him to her.

# NINE

AEGEUS, King of the Athenians, had been a strong man. Age whitened his hair and beard, shrank the muscles around the big bones, dimmed his eyes, knotted his fingers with arthritis. But still he sat his throne in dignity; and when he handled the twin hemispheres of the *mentatór*, he showed no fear.

The slave who had learned Keftiu from it groveled on the rush-strewn clay floor. He could not speak his new language clearly, his mouth being torn and puffed from the blow of a spearbutt that overcame his first struggling, screaming terror. The warriors—Aegeus' guards and chance visitors, about fifty altogether—stood firm; but many a tongue was moistening lips, many an eyeball rolled beneath a sweaty brow. Servants and women cowered back against the walls. The dogs, giant mastiffs and wolfhounds, sensed fear and growled.

"This is a mighty gift," the king said.

"We hope it will be of service, my lord," Reid answered.

"It will. But the power in it is more: a guardian, an omen. Let these helmets be kept in the Python shrine. Ten days hence, let there be a sacrifice of dedication, and three days of feasting and games. As for these four who have brought the gift, know every man that they are royal guests. Let them be given suitable quarters, raiment, comely women, and whatever else they may lack. Let all pay them honor."

Aegeus leaned forward on the lionskin that covered his marble throne. Peering to see the newcomers better, he finished less solemnly, "You must be wearied. Would you not like to be shown your rooms, be washed, take refreshment and rest? This evening we shall dine with you and hear your stories in fullness."

His son Theseus, who occupied a lower seat on his right, nodded. "So be it," he ordered. Otherwise the prince's countenance remained unmoving, his gaze wary.

A slave chamberlain took over. As his party was led from the hall, Reid had a chance to look around more closely than hitherto. Athens, smaller, poorer, further from civilization, did not boast the stone architecture of a Mycenae or Tiryns. The royal palace on the heights of the Acropolis was wood. But those were enormous timbers, in this age before the deforestation of Greece. Massive columns upheld beams and rafters down a length of easily a hundred feet. Windows, their shutters now open, admitted some daylight from a clerestory, as did the smokehole in the shake roof. But it was gloomy in here; shields and weapons hung behind the benches already threw back the glimmer of stone lamps. Yet furs, tapestries, gold and silver vessels made a rude magnificence.

Three wings ran from the hall. One was for utility and servitors' quarters, one for the royal family and its permanent freeborn attendants, one for guests. The rooms, fronting on a corridor, were cubicles, their doorways closed merely by drapes. However, those drapes were thick and lavishly patterned; the plaster walls were ornamented with more tapestries; the bedsteads were heaped with sheepskins and furs above the straw; next to rhytons stood generous containers of wine as well as water; and in each compartment a girl made timid obeisance.

Oleg clapped his hands. "Oh, ho!" he chortled. "I like this place!"

"If we never get back," Uldin agreed, "we could do far worse than become Aegeus' men."

The chamberlain indicated a room for Erissa. "Uh, she and I are together," Reid said. "One *servant* will be ample."

The other man leered. "You get one apiece, master. So 'twas commanded. They can share the extra room. We've not much company, what with harvest season ashore and fall weather afloat." He was a bald-headed Illyrian with the perkiness of any old retainer. —No, Reid thought suddenly. He's a slave. He behaves like a lifer who's at last become a trusty in his prison.

The girls said they would fetch the promised garments. Was food desired? Did our lord and lady wish to be taken to the bathhouse, scrubbed, massaged, and rubbed with olive oil by their humble attendants?

"Later," Erissa said. "In time to have us ready for the king's feast—and the queen's," she added, for Achaean women did not dine formally with men. "First we would rest."

When she and Reid were alone, she laid arms around him, cheek against his shoulder, and whispered forlornly, "What can we do?"

"I don't know," he replied into the sunny odor of her hair. "So far we've had scant choice, haven't we? We may end our days here. As our friends said, there are worse fates."

Her clasp tightened till the nails dug into his back. "You can't mean that. These are the folk who burned—who will burn Knossos and end the peace of the Minos—so they can be free to go pirating!"

He didn't answer directly, for he was thinking: That's how she looks at it. Me, I don't know. They're rough, the Achaeans, but aren't they open and upright in their fashion? And what about those human victims for the Minotaur?

Aloud he said, "Well, if nothing else, I can arrange your passage to Keftiu territory."

"Without you?" She drew apart from him. Strangeness rose in her voice. Her look caught his and would not let go. "It will not be, Duncan. You will fare to Atlantis, and love me, and in Knossos you will beget our son. Afterward—"

"Hush!" Alarmed, he laid a hand across her mouth. Diores, at least, was probably quite capable of planting spies on the king's mysterious visitors, the more so when one of them was a Cretan of rank. And the door drape wasn't soundproof. Too late, Reid regretted not using the *mentatór* to give his party a language unknown here. Hunnish or Old Russian would have done quite well.

But in the desert they'd been too distracted to foresee a need; and maybe Diores would have forbidden magic on his ship; yes, doubtless he would have, if only to prevent those whom he was suspicious of from gaining that advantage.

"These are, uh, matters too sacred to speak of here," Reid said. "Let's seek a private place later."

Erissa nodded. "Yes. I understand. Soon." Her lips writhed. She blinked hard. "Too soon. However long our fate will be in taking us, it will be too soon." Drawing him toward the bed: "You are not overwearied, are you? This while that we have together?"

The slave who brought them breakfast in the morning, leftovers from last night's roast ox, announced, "Prince Theseus asks the pleasure of my lord's company. My lady is invited to spend the day with the queen and her girls." She had an accent; what homeland did she yearn for?

Erissa wrinkled her nose at Reid. She was in for a dull time, even if the girls were from noble families, learning housewifery as attendants on Aegeus' consort. (She was his fourth in succession but would doubtless outlive him, he being too old to bring her to her grave of a dozen children beginning when she was fifteen.) Reid signed her to accept. Why give needless offense to touchy hosts?

The tunic, cloak, sandals, and Phrygian cap he donned were presents from Theseus' wardrobe. Tall though the Achaeans were, few reached the six feet common in Reid's well-nourished milieu. The prince actually topped the American by a couple of inches. The latter had been surprised at the degree of surprise this caused him, till he tracked down the reason: Mary Renault's fine novels, which described Theseus as a short man. Well, she'd made—would make—a logical interpretation of the legend; but how much of the legend would reflect truth? For that matter, had this Aegeus and Theseus any identity with the father and son of the tradition?

They must, Reid thought hopelessly. Their names are associated with the fall of Knossos and the conquest of Crete. And Knossos *will* fall, Crete *will* be overrun, in our very near future, when Atlantis goes down.

The bronze sword he hung at his waist was from Aegeus, leaf-shaped, well-balanced, lovely and deadly. He could not fault the royal pair for stinginess.

He found Theseus waiting in the hall. Except for slaves tidying up, it felt cavernously empty and still after last evening's carousal. (Torch-flare; fire roaring on a central hearthstone less loudly than the chants, footstampings, lyres and syrinxes and drums, shouts and brags that filled the smoky air; dogs snapping after bones flung them off threstle tables; servants scurrying to keep the winecups filled; and through it all, Theseus seated impassive, quietly questioning the strangers.) "Rejoice, my lord," Reid greeted.

"Rejoice." The prince lifted a muscle-corded arm. "I thought you might like to be shown our countryside."

"You are most kind, my lord. Ah . . . my friends—?"

"My captain Diores is taking the warriors Uldin and Oleg to his estate. He's promised them horses, and they in turn have promised to show the use of that saddle with footrests which Uldin brought."

And he'll pump them, Reid reflected, and he'll try to split them off from Erissa and me. . . . Stirrups weren't invented till millennia after this, were they? I read that somewhere. They were what made heavy cavalry possible. Suppose they catch on, here and now—what then?

Can time be changed? Does Erissa's Thalassocracy have to die? Must I really leave her, in an eerie kind of incest, for her younger self?

If not . . . will the future grow into a different shape from what I knew? Will my Pamela ever be born? Will I?

He tried to summon his wife's image and found that harder to do than it should have been, these few days after he was lost from her.

Theseus said, "Come," and led the way outside. He was broad in proportion to his height, but he walked lightly. Fair-skinned, tawny of hair and beard, his blunt-nosed, full-lipped features were handsome. The eyes were remarkable, set well apart and of an amber hue, leonine eyes. For the outing he had exchanged his gaudily embroidered festive garments for plain gray wool. He kept his golden headband, though, the golden brooch at his throat and bracelet on his thick wrist.

While the wind was brisk outdoors, it was not yet an autumn gale, and the clouds it sent scudding were white. Their shadows swept over a huge landscape, mountains to north and northwest, the Saronic Gulf to the south and west. Across those few miles, against blue-green whitecaps, Reid made out a cluster he could recognize as boathouses and beached ships at the Piraeus. A dirt road from there to here cut a brown streak through stubblefields and dusty-green olive orchards. The whole Attic plain was similarly dappled with agriculture. At a distance he noticed two large houses and their outbuildings that must belong to wealthy men, and numerous smallholder cottages. Groves of oak or poplar usually surrounded them. The mountains were densely forested. This was not his Greece.

He noticed how full of birds the sky was. Most he couldn't name except in general terms, different kinds of thrush, dove, duck, heron, hawk, swan, crow. Thus far men hadn't ruined nature. Sparrows hopped among the courtyard cobblestones. Besides dogs, the animals were absent that would have wandered around a farm, swine, donkeys, sheep, goats, cows, chickens, geese. But workers bustled among the buildings which defined the enclosure. A household this big required plenty of labor, cleaning, cooking, milling, baking, brewing, spinning, weaving, endlessly. Most of the staff were women, and most had young children near their bare feet or clinging to their worn shifts: the next generation of slaves. However, several industries were carried on by men. Through open shed doors, Reid glimpsed in action a smithy, a ropewalk, a tannery, a potter's wheel, a carpenter shop.

"Are these all slaves, my lord?" he asked.

"Not all," Theseus said. "Particularly, it's not wise to keep many unfree males about. We hire them, mostly Athenians, a few skilled foreigners." He grinned, his grin that never seemed to reach deeper than his teeth. "They're encouraged to breed brats on our bondwomen. Thus everyone's happy."

Except maybe the bondwomen, Reid thought, the more so when their boys are sold away.

Theseus scowled. "We have to keep a Cretan clerk. No need; we've men who can write, aye, men whose forebears taught the Cretans to write! But the Minos requires it of us."

To keep track of income and outgo, Reid deduced, partly for purposes of assessing tribute, partly for indications of what the Athenians may be up to. Say, what's this about the Achaeans being literate before the Minoans were? That doesn't make sense.

Theseus halted his complaint before he should grow indiscreet. "I thought we'd drive out to my own farmstead," he suggested. "You can see a good bit on the way, and for myself I want to make sure the threshing and storing are well in hand."

"I'd enjoy that, my lord."

The stable was the sole stone building, no doubt because horses were too valuable and loved to risk to fire. Not as big as their twentieth-century counterparts, they nevertheless were mettlesome animals which whickered softly and nuzzled Theseus' palm when he stroked them. "Hitch Stamper and Longtail to the everyday chariot," he ordered the head groom. "No, don't summon a driver. I'll take 'em."

Two men could stand on the flat bed of the car, behind a bronze front and sides decorated with bas-reliefs. In war Theseus, armored, would have kept his place behind a near-naked youth who had the reins, himself wielding spear and sword against enemy infantry. Reid decided that was a skill which could only be acquired by training from babyhood. He had everything he could do just hanging on in the unsprung conveyance.

Theseus flicked whip over the horses and they clattered out. The twin wheels squeaked and rumbled. Even lacking ball bearings, it didn't seem like much of a load for a pair of animals to draw. Then Reid noticed the choking chest-strap harness. What if Oleg made a horse collar?

Athens clustered nearly to the top of steep, rocky Acropolis Hill. It was a fair-sized city by present-day standards; Reid guessed at twenty or thirty thousand inhabitants, though a floating population from the hinterland and foreign parts might raise that figure. (He asked Theseus and got a quizzical stare. The Achaeans kept close track of many things, but counting people had not occurred to them.) Much of the settled area lay outside the defensive walls, indicating rapid growth. Buildings were adobe, flat-roofed, often three or four stories high, jammed along narrow, unpaved, crazily twisting streets. In those lanes Reid did see hogs, competing with mongrels, mice, roaches, and clouds of flies for the offal tossed from houses.

"Make way!" Theseus trumpeted. "Make way!"

They parted for him, the warriors, craftsmen, merchants, mariners, innkeepers, shopkeepers, scribes, laborers, prostitutes, housewives, children, hierophants, and Lord knew what whose movement and babble brought the city to life. Glimpses remained with Reid: A woman, one hand supporting a water jug on her head, one lifting her skirts above the muck. A gaunt donkey, overburdened with faggots, lashed forward by its countryman owner. A booth where a sandalmaker sat crying his wares. Another booth where a typically intricate bargain had just been struck, payment to be made partly in kind and partly in an agreed-on weight of metal. A coppersmith at work, shutting the whole world out of his head except for his hammer and the adze he was forging. An open winehouse door and a drunken sailor telling lengthy lies about the perils he had survived. Two little boys, naked, playing what looked remarkably like hop-scotch. A portly burgher, apprentices around him to protect him from jostling. A squat, dark, bearded man in robe and high-crowned brimless hat who must be from Asia Minor . . . no, here they simply called it Asia. . . .

The chariot rattled by that plateau, where several wooden temples stood, which would later be known as the Areopagus. It passed through a gateway in the city wall, whose roughly dressed stonework was inferior to the Mycenaean ruins Reid had once visited. (Now he wondered how long after Pamela's day it would be before Seattle or Chicago lay tumbled, in silence broken only by crickets.) Beyond the "suburbs" the horses came onto a rutted road and Theseus let them trot.

Reid clung to the rail. He hoped his knees wouldn't be jolted backward or the teeth shaken out of his jaws.

Theseus noticed. He drew his beasts to a walk. They shimmied impatiently but obeyed. The prince looked around. "You're not used to this, are you?" he asked.

"No, my lord. We . . . travel otherwise in my country."

"Riding?"

"Well, yes. And, uh, in wagons that have springs to absorb the shock." Reid was faintly surprised to learn, out of his knowledge, that the Achaeans had a word for springs. Checking more closely, he found he had said "metal bowstaves."

"Hm," Theseus grunted. "Such must be costly. And don't they soon wear out?"

"We use iron, my lord. Iron's both cheaper and stronger than bronze when you know how to obtain and work it. The ores are far more plentiful than those of copper or tin."

"Yes, so Oleg told me yesterday when I examined his gear. Do you know the secret?"

"I fear not, my lord. It's no secret in my country, but it doesn't happen to be my work. I, well, plan buildings."

"Might your companions know?"

"Perhaps." Reid thought that, given a chance to experiment,

he could probably reconstruct the process himself. The basic idea was to apply a mechanical blast to your furnace, thus making the fire sufficiently hot to reduce the element, and afterward to alloy and temper the product until it became steel. Oleg might well have dropped in on such an operation in his era and observed equipment he could easily imitate.

They drove unspeaking for a while. At this pace it wasn't hard to keep balanced, though impacts still ran up the shinbones. The clatter of wheels was nearly lost in the noise of the wind, where it soughed among poplars lining the road. It cuffed with chilly hands and sent cloaks flapping. A flight of crows beat against it. The sun made their blackness look polished, until a cloud swept past and for a moment brilliance went out of the landscape. Smoke streamed flat from the roof of a peasant's clay house. Women stooped in his wheatfield, reaping it with sickles. The wind pressed their coarse brown gowns against their flanks. Two men followed them, shocking; as they moved along, they would pick up their spears and shift those too.

Theseus half turned, reins negligently in his right hand, so that his yellow eyes could rest on Reid. "Your tale is more eldritch than any I ever thought to hear," he said.

The American smiled wryly. "It is to me also."

"Borne on a whirlwind across the world, from lands so distant we've gotten no whisper about them, by the car of a magician—do you truly believe that was sheer happenstance? That there's no destiny in you?"

"I . . . don't . . . think there is, my lord."

"Diores tells me you four spoke oddly about having come out of time as well as space." The deep voice was level but unrelenting; the free hand rested on a sword pommel. "What does that mean?"

Here it comes, Reid told himself. Though his tongue was somewhat dry, he got his rehearsed answer out steadily enough. "We're not sure either, my lord. Imagine how bewildered we were and are. And we're confused as to reckoning. That's natural, isn't it? Our countries have no common reign or event to count from. I wondered if perhaps the wizard's wagon had crossed both miles and years. It was only a wondering and I don't really know."

He dared not make an outright denial. Too many hints had been dropped or might be dropped. Theseus and Diores were no more ignorant of the nature of time than Reid; everywhere and everywhen, mystery has the same size. The concept of chrono-kinesis should not be unthinkable to them, who were used to oracles, prophets, and stories about predestined dooms.

Then why not tell them the whole truth? Because of Erissa.

Theseus' tone roughened: "I'd be less worried if that Cretan didn't share your bed."

"My lord," Reid protested, "she was swept along like the rest of us, by meaningless chance."

"Will you set her aside, then?"

"No," Reid said, "I can't," and wondered if that was not the bedrock fact. He added in haste, "Our sufferings have made a bond between us. Surely you, my lord, wouldn't forsake a comrade. And aren't you at peace with Crete?"

"In a way," Theseus answered. "For a while."

He stood motionless, drawn into himself, until suddenly:

"Hear me, my guest Duncan. I say nothing to your dishonor, but an outlander such as you is easily hoodwinked. Let me tell you how things really are.

"The reality is that Crete sits at this end of the Midworld Sea like a spider in its web, and the Hellenic tribes grow weary of being flies trapped and bloodsucked. Every realm of us in reach of a coastline must bend the knee, pay the tribute, send the hostages, keep no more ships than the Minos allows nor carry out any venture the Minos disallows. We want our freedom."

"Forgive this outlander, my lord," Reid dared say, "but doesn't the tribute—timber, grain, goods that set the Cretans free to do other things than produce them, I suppose—doesn't it buy you protection from piracy, and so help rather than hinder you?"

Theseus snorted. " 'Piracy' is what the Minos says it is. Why should our young men not be let blood themselves, and win their fortunes off a Levantine tin ship or a Hittite town? Because it would inconvenience the Cretans in their trade relationships with those places, that's why." He paused. "More to the point, maybe, why should my father or I not be allowed to unite Attica? Why should other Achaean kings not bring their own kinfolk together in like wise? It wouldn't take much warring. But no, the Minos prevents it by a net of treaties—to keep the 'barbarians' divided and therefore weak," he fleered. The word he used had the connotation of the English "backward natives."

"A balance of power—" Reid attempted.

"And the Minos holding the scales! Listen. Northward and eastward, in the mountains, are the real barbarians. They prowl the marches like wolves. If we Achaeans cannot be brought together, in the end we'll be invaded and overrun. What then of 'preserving civilization,' when the scrolls burn with the cities?

"Civilization," Theseus continued after a moment. "Are we such oafs born that we can't take our fair part in it? They were Argives who decided the old priestly script of Crete was too cumbersome and devised a new one, so much better that now probably half the clerks in Knossos are Argives."

There was the answer to the riddle of Linear A and Linear B, Reid thought faintly. No conquest by Homeric Greeks—not yet —simply adoption of a desirable foreign invention, like Europe taking numerals from the Arabs or wallpaper from the Chinese or kayaks from the Eskimos—or he himself, bound for Japan. Evidently quite a few Achaeans were resident in Knossos, and no doubt in other Cretan towns. Scribes expert in Linear B would naturally be hired from among them, and the scribes would naturally prefer to use their own language, which the script best fitted.

A potential fifth column?

"Not that I personally believe that's any great thing," Theseus said. "Punching marks on clay tablets or scribbling on papyrus is no fit work for a man."

"What is, my lord?" Reid asked.

"To plow, sow, reap, build, hunt, sail, make war, make love, make a strong home for his kin and an honored name for his descendants. And for us who are kings, also to raise up and defend the kingdom."

A horse shied. Theseus needed a minute with reins and whip to bring the team under control. Afterward he drove two-handed, eyes straight before him, talking in a monotone that blew back over his shoulder:

"Let me tell you the story. It's no secret. Some fifty years ago the Kalydonians and certain allies launched an expedition which fell on southern Crete and sacked a number of towns, harrying so well that these have not since been rebuilt. They could do this because of secret preparations and because three weak, pleasure-loving Minoses in a row had neglected the navy. Crete's been well logged by now, you see, so ship timber must be imported as you guessed, at the expense of luxuries.

"But a new admiral got command. Next year he whipped the Kalydonians with what vessels he had. A new Minos came to the throne soon after and helped this Admiral Rheakles strengthen the fleet. They decided between them to bring under control all Achaeans who had seaports and hence might threaten the Thalassocracy. This they did, partly by outright conquest, partly by playing us off against each other.

"Well, seven and twenty years ago, my father Aegeus sought to end his vassalage and unite Attica. He revolted. It was put down. The Minos let him remain as under-king, to avoid a protracted war that might have spread, but laid harsh terms on him. Among other conditions, every nine years, seven youths and seven maidens of our noblest families must go to Knossos, living as hostages till the next lot arrives."

"What?" Reid asked. "They're not . . . sacrificed to the Minotaur?"

Theseus cast him a glance. "What're you talking about? The Minotaur is the sacrifice. Don't you see the cunning of the scheme? The hostages leave here at their most impressionable age. They come home grown, ready to join our most important councils and continue our most powerful houses—but dyed for life in Cretan colors.

"Well. Even that far back, Diores was a shrewd adviser. Without him we'd have gotten worse peace terms than we did. Now my father had no living sons, and my uncle's were among the first hostages chosen, of course. Diores urged my father to go to Troezen, at the end of the Argolis peninsula. Its king was his kinsman and an old ally. He agreed to the plan, that my father should secretly beget an heir on a daughter of his. I was that heir."

It wouldn't be impossible to keep such an operation confidential, Reid reflected, in this world of tenuous communications between realms often separated by trackless wildernesses.

"I was raised in Troezen," Theseus said. "It also was tributary to Crete, but being poor, it rarely saw a Cretan. —Poor? In manhood we were rich. Before the first beard bloomed on my cheeks I was helping clear bandits and roving beasts out of the hinterlands.

"Diores often came visiting. Five years back he brought me to Athens. I claimed the heirship; my Cretan-loving cousins denied me it; my party'd kept their swords loose in the scabbards; and afterward the Minos could do nothing."

Or would do nothing, Reid thought. Does an empire mainly interested in keeping peace along its borders and trade lanes ever pay close attention to dynastic quarrels among the tribes it's holding in check . . . until the day when, too late, it wishes it had done so?

"What are your plans, my lord?" he felt he might ask.

Heavy shoulders rose and fell beneath the tossing cloak. "To do what seems best. I'll tell you this, Duncan: I'm not ignorant of what goes on in the Thalassocracy. I've been there. And not only as a royal visitor, fed buttered words and shown what the courtiers want me to see. No, I've fared under different names as trader or deckhand. I've looked, listened, met people, learned."

Again Theseus turned to regard Reid with those disturbing eyes. "Mind you," he said, "I've spoken no dangerous word today.

They know in Knossos we're restless on the mainland. They know, too, as long as their warships outnumber those that they let all the Achaeans together keep, they're safe. So they don't mind if we grumble. They'll even throw us a bone now and then, since we do provide them trade and tribute and a buffer against the mountaineers. I've told you nothing that the Cretan resident and his clerk in the palace haven't often heard—nothing I didn't say to the Minos' own first minister, that time I paid my official visit to Knossos."

"I'd not denounce you, surely, my lord," Reid answered, wishing he were more of a diplomat.

"You're something new in the game," Theseus growled. "Your powers, your knowledge, whatever destiny hovers above you—who knows? At least I want you to have the truth."

The truth as you see it, Reid thought. Which is not the truth Erissa sees. Me, I'm still a blind man.

"I fret over what your Cretan leman may whisper to you," Theseus said. "Or do to you by her arts. Diores warns me she's a weird creature, closer than most to the All-Mother."

"I . . . did not know . . . you worshipped her Goddess, my lord."

Like sundown in a desert, the hardheaded statecraft dropped from Theseus, primitive dread fell upon him, and he whispered, "She is very mighty, very old. Could I but find an oracle to tell me She's only the wife of Father Zeus— Hoy!" he yelled to his horses, and cracked the whip across them. "Get going there!" The chariot rocked.

# TEN

THE CHANCE to talk privately came three days afterward, when Diores brought Oleg and Uldin back to Athens. They had been days of total fascination for Reid, a torrent of sights, sounds, smells, songs, stories, sudden explosive realizations of what this myth or that line of poetry really signified. And the nights—by tacit agreement, he and Erissa put no word about their fate into their whisperings at night. For the time being, anxiety, culture shock, even homesickness were largely anesthetized in him.

The Russian and the Hun had been still better off. Oleg bubbled about the chances he saw to make innovations, especially in shipbuilding and metallurgy, and thus to make a fortune. In his dour fashion, Uldin registered enthusiasms of his own. Attica held an abundance of swift, spirited horses at the right age for breaking to the saddle and of young men interested in experimenting with cavalry. Give him a few years, he said, and he'd have a troop that nothing could stand against when they rode off a-conquering.

This was related in the hall before Aegeus, Theseus, Diores, and the leading guardsmen. Reid cleared his throat. "You suppose we can never return to our countries, don't you?" he said.

"How can we?" Uldin retorted.

"It must be talked over." Reid braced himself. "My lord king, we four have much to decide between us, not least how we can try to show you our gratitude. It won't be easy to reach agreement, as unlike as we are. I fear it would be impossible in the hustle and bustle of this establishment. You won't think ill of us, will you, my lord, if we go off alone?"

Aegeus hesitated. Theseus frowned. Diores smiled and said smoothly, "Zeus thunder me, no! Tell you what I'll do. Tomorrow I'll have a wagon ready, nice comfortable seats, a stock o' food and drink, and a trusty warrior to drive her wherever you like." He lifted his palm. "No, don't deny me, friends. I insist. Nothing's too good for shipmates o' mine. Wouldn't be sensible to leave with a good-looking woman and just two o' you who can handle a blade."

And that, Reid thought grimly, was that. They would never be allowed to talk in private.

But when he told Erissa, she was undismayed for some reason.

The fall weather continued pleasant, crisp air, sunshine picking out the gold of summer-dried grass and the hues of such leaves as had started faintly to turn. The wagon, mule-drawn, was indeed easy to ride in. The driver was a big young man named Peneleos, who addressed his passengers courteously though his glance upon them was ice-blue. Reid felt sure that, besides muscles, he had been chosen for especially keen ears and a knowledge of Keftiu.

"Where to?" he asked as they rumbled from the palace.

"A quiet spot," Erissa said before anybody else could speak. "A place to rest alone."

"M-m, the Grove of Periboea? We can get there about when you'll want your midday bread. If you're a votaress of Her, my lady, as I've been told, you'll know what we should do so the nymph won't mind."

"Yes. Marvelous." Erissa turned to Oleg. "Tell me about Diores' farm. About everything! I've been penned. No complaint against the most gracious queen, of course. Achaean ways are not Cretan."

She has a scheme, Reid realized. His pulse picked up.

Keeping the conversation neutral was no problem. They had a near infinity of memories to trade, from their homes as well as from here. But even had the case been different, Reid knew Erissa would have managed. She wasn't coquettish; she drew Oleg, Uldin, and Peneleos out by asking intelligent questions and making comments that sparked replies. ("If your ships, Oleg, are so much sturdier than ours that the . . . Norsemen, did you say? . . . actually cross the River Ocean—is that because you've harder wood, or iron for nails and braces, or what?") Then she listened to the reply, leaning close. It was impossible to be unaware of her sculptured features, sea-changeable eyes, lips slightly parted over white teeth, slim throat, and of how the light burnished her hair and the wind pulled her Achaean gown tight around breasts and waist.

She knows men, Reid thought. How she knows them!

The sacred grove was a stand of laurel trees surrounding a

small meadow. In the center lay a huge boulder whose shape, vaguely suggestive of a yoni, must account for the demigoddess Periboea. To one side stretched an olive orchard, on the other a barley field, both harvested and deserted. In the background Mount Hymettus dreamed beneath the sun. The trees broke the wind in a lullaby rustle, the sere grass was thick and warm. Here dwelt peace.

Erissa knelt, said a prayer, divided a loaf of bread and laid a portion on the boulder for the nymph to give her birds. Rising, she said, "We are welcome. Bring our food and wine from the wagon. And Peneleos, won't you remove that helmet and breastplate? We can see anybody coming miles away; and it's not meet to carry weapons before a female deity."

"I beg her forgiveness," the guardsman said. He was less chagrined than he was glad to take off his burden and relax. They enjoyed a frugal, friendly lunch.

"Well, we were going to talk over our plans," Uldin said afterward.

"Not yet," Erissa answered. "I've had a better idea. The nymph is well disposed toward us. If we lie down and sleep awhile, she may send us a dream for guidance."

Peneleos shifted about where he sat. "I'm not sleepy," he said. "Besides, my duty—"

"Of course. Yet you also have a duty to learn for your king what you can of these strange matters. True?"

"M-m-m . . . yes."

"It may be that she will favor you above us, this being your country and not ours. Surely she'll be pleased if you show her the respect of inviting her counsel. Come." Erissa took his hand. He rose to her gentle tugging. "Over here. On the sunlit side of the rock. Sit down, lean back, feel her warmth. And now—" She drew from her bosom a small bronze mirror. "Now look into this token of the Goddess, Who is the Mother of nymphs."

She knelt before him. He stared bemusedly at her and the shining disk and back. "No," she murmured. "The mirror only,

Peneleos, wherein you will see that which She wills." She turned it slowly.

Good Lord! thought Reid. He drew Oleg and Uldin away, behind the big stone.

"What's she doing?" the Russian inquired uneasily.

"Hsh," Reid whispered. "Sit. Be quiet. This is a holy thing."

"A heathen thing, I fear." Oleg crossed himself. But he and the Hun obeyed.

Sunlight poured through murmurous leaves. The sweet smell of dried grass lifted like smoke to meet it. Bees hummed among briar roses. Erissa crooned.

When she came around the boulder, none of her morning's cheerfulness was left. She had laid that aside. Her look was at once grave and exalted. The white streak in her hair stood forth against its darkness like a crown.

Reid got to his feet. "You've done it?" he asked.

She nodded. "He will not awaken before I command. Afterward he will think he drowsed off with the rest of us and had whatever dream I will have related to him." She gave the American a close regard. "I did not know you knew of the Sleep."

"What witchcraft is this?" Oleg rasped.

Hypnotism, Reid named it to himself. Except that she has more skill in it than any therapist I ever heard of in my own era. Well, I suppose that's a matter of personality.

"It is the Sleep," Erissa said, "that I lay on the sick when it can ease their pain and on the haunted to drive their nightmares out of them. It does not always come when I wish. But Peneleos is a simple fellow and I spent the trip here putting him at ease."

Uldin nodded. "I've watched shamans do what you did," he remarked. "Have no fears, Oleg. Though I never awaited meeting a she-shaman."

"Now let us speak," Erissa said.

Her sternness brought home to Reid like a sword thrust that she was not really the frightened castaway, yearning exile, ardent and wistful mistress he had imagined he knew. Those were waves on a deep sea. She had indeed become a stranger to the girl who remembered him—a slave who won free, a wanderer who stayed alive among savages, a queen in the strong household she herself had brought to being, a healer, witch, priestess and prophetess. Suddenly he had an awesome feeling that her triune Goddess had in all truth entered this place and possessed her.

"What is the doom of Atlantis?" she went on.

Reid stooped and poured himself a cup of wine to help him swallow his dread. "You don't recall?" he mumbled.

"Not the end. The months before, yours and mine, on the holy island and in Knossos, those are unforgotten. But I will not speak of what I now know will be for you even as it was for me. That is too sacred.

"I will say this: I have questioned out what year this is, and put together such numbers as the years since the present Minos ascended his throne or since the war between Crete and Athens. From these I have reckoned that we are four-and-twenty years from that day when I am borne out of Rhodes to Egypt. You will soon depart hence, Duncan."

Oleg's ruddiness had paled. Uldin had retreated into stolidity.

Reid gulped the sharp red wine. He didn't look at Erissa; his gaze took refuge on Mount Hymettus above the treetops. "What is the last you clearly remember?" he asked.

"We went to Knossos in spring, we sisters of the rite. I danced with the bulls." Her measured, impersonal tone softened. "Afterward you came, and we— But Theseus was already there, and others I cannot remember well. Maybe I was too happy to care. Our happiness does live on within me." Quieter yet: "It will live as long as I do, and I will take it home with me to the Goddess."

Again she was the wise-woman in council: "We need a clearer foreknowledge than my clouded recollections of the end, or the tales about it that I gathered later, can give us. What have you to tell?"

Reid gripped the cup till his fingers hurt. "Your Atlantis," he said, "is that not a volcanic island about sixty miles north of Crete?"

"Yes. I believe the smoke rising from the mountain, as it often does, brought about the name 'Land of the Pillar.' Atlantis is the seat of the Ariadne, who reigns over rites and votaries throughout the realm even as the Minos reigns over worldly affairs."

Ariadne? Not a name, as myth was to make it, but a title: "Most Sacred One."

"I know Atlantis will sink in fire, ash, storm, and destruction," Erissa said.

"Then you know everything I do, or nearly," Reid answered in wretchedness. "My age had nothing but shards. It happened too long ago."

He had read a few popular accounts of the theorizing and excavating that had begun in earnest in his own day. A cluster of islands, Thera and its still tinier companions, the Santorini group, had looked insignificant except for being remnants left by an eruption that once dwarfed Krakatoa. But lately several scientists—yes, Anghelos Galanopoulos in the lead—had started wondering. If you reconstructed the single original island, you got a picture oddly suggestive of the capital of Atlantis as described by Plato; and ancient walls were known to be buried under the lava and cinders. That settlement might be better preserved than Pompeii, what parts had not vanished in the catastrophe.

To be sure, Plato could simply have been embellishing his discourses in the *Timaios* and the *Kritias* with a fiction. He had put his lost continent in midocean, impossibly big and impossibly far back if it was to have fought Athens. Yet there was some reason to believe he drew on a tradition, that half-memory of the Minoan empire which flickered through classical legend.

Assume his figures were in error. He claimed to derive the story from Solon, who had it from an Egyptian priest, who said he drew on records in another, older language. Translating from Egyptian to Greek numerals, you could easily get numbers above one hundred wrong by a factor of ten; and a timespan counted in months could be garbled into the same amount of years.

Plato was logically forced to move his Atlantis beyond the Pillars of Hercules. The Mediterranean didn't have room for it. But take away the obviously invented hinterland. Shrink the city plan by one order of magnitude. The outline became not too different from that of Santorini. Change years to months. The date of Atlantis' death shifted to between 1500 and 1300 B.C.

And this bestrode the 1400 B.C.—give or take a few decades—that archeologists assigned to the destruction of Knossos, the fall of the Thalassocracy.]

Reid thought: I cannot tell her that I found what I read interesting, but not interesting enough to make me go there or even to read further.

"What are you talking about?" Uldin barked.

"We know the island will founder," Reid told him. "That will be the most terrible thing ever to happen in this part of the world. A mountain will burst, stones and ashes rain from heaven, the darkness spread as far as Egypt. The waves that are raised will sink the Cretan fleet; and Crete has no other defenses. Earthquakes will shake its cities apart. The Achaeans will be free to enter as conquerors."

They pondered it, there in the curious peace of the sanctuary. Wind lulled, bees buzzed. Finally Oleg, eyes almost hidden beneath contracted yellow brows, asked, "Why won't the Achaean ships be sunk too?"

"They're further off," Uldin guessed.

"No," Erissa said. "Over the years I heard accounts. Vessels were swamped, flung ashore and smashed, and coasts flooded beneath a wall of water, along the whole Peloponnesus and the west coast of Asia. Not the Athenian fleet, though. It was at sea and suffered little. Theseus boasted to the end of his life how Poseidon had fought for him."

Reid nodded. He knew something about tsunamis. "The water rose beneath the hulls, but bore them while it did," he said. "A wave like that is actually quite gentle at sea. I imagine the Cretans were in harbor, or near the shores they were supposed to defend. Caught on the incoming billow, they were borne to land."

"Like being in heavy surf." Oleg shivered beneath the sun.

"A thousand times worse," Reid said.

"When is this to happen?" Uldin asked.

"Early next year," Erissa told him.

"She means in the springtime," Reid explained, since Russia would use a different calendar from hers and the Huns, perhaps, none.

"Well," Oleg said after a silence. "Well."

He lumbered to the woman and awkwardly patted her shoulder. "I'm sorry for your folk," he said. "Can nothing be done?"

"Who can stay the demons?" Uldin responded. Erissa was staring past them all.

"The Powers have been kind to us," the Hun continued. "Here we are on the side that'll win."

"No!" flared Erissa. Fists clenched, she brought her eyes back to the men; the gaze burned. "It will not be. We can warn the Minos and the Ariadne. Let Atlantis and the coastal cities on Crete be evacuated. Let the fleet stand out to sea. And . . . contrive to keep the cursed Athenian ships home. Then the realm will live."

"Who'll believe us?" Reid breathed.

"Can what is foredoomed be changed?" Oleg asked as softly and shakenly. His fingers flew, tracing crosses.

Uldin hunched his shoulders. "*Should* it be?" he demanded.

"What?" Reid asked in shock.

"What's wrong with the Achaeans winning?" Uldin said. "They're a healthy folk. And the Powers favor them. Who but a madman would fight against that?"

"Hold on," Oleg said, deep in his throat. "You speak what could be dangerous."

Erissa said, unperturbed, like embodied destiny, "We must

try. We will try. I know." To Reid: "Before long, you will know too."

"Anyhow," the architect added, "Atlantis holds our only chance of ever getting home."

# *ELEVEN*

RAIN CAME THAT EVENING, racing before a gale. It hammered on walls, hissed down off roofs, gurgled among cobblestones. The wind hooted and rattled doors and shutters. Clay braziers within the hall could not drive out a dank chill, nor could lamps, torches, and hearthfire hold night far off. Shadows crouched on the rafters and jumped misshapen across the warriors who sat along the benches, mutedly talking, casting uneasy glances at the group around the thrones.

Aegeus huddled in a bearskin and hardly spoke. The royal word was given by Theseus, massive on his right, and Diores who stood on his left. Of those who confronted them, standing, Oleg and Uldin likewise kept silence.

Reid and Gathon had had no beforehand conference; they had barely met, when protocol demanded that the remarkable newcomers be presented to the Voice of the Minos; but the instant he trod through the door and took off his drenched cloak, the Cretan's glance had met the American's and they were allies.

"What business with me was too urgent to wait until morning?" Gathon inquired after the formalities.

He spoke politely but gave no deference, for he represented Aegeus' overlord. Less than a viceroy, more than an ambassador, he observed, he reported to Knossos, he saw to it that the terms of Athenian vassalage were carried out. In looks he was purely Cretan: fine-featured, with large dark eyes, still slender in middle age. His curly black hair was banged across the forehead;

two braids in front of the ears and carefully combed tresses behind fell halfway to his waist. As well as tweezers and a
sickle-shaped bronze razor permitted, he was clean-shaven. More
out of consideration for the weather than for mainland sensi-
bilities, he had left the plain kilt of his people for an ankle-
length pleated robe. The garment looked Egyptian; the lands
of Pharaoh and Minos had long been closely tied.

Theseus leaned forward. Firelight played across his sinewy
countenance and in the carnivore eyes. "Our guests wished to
see you as soon as might be," he stated, rough-toned. "They told
us of an oracle."

"The Goddess' business does not wait," Reid declared. Erissa
had described the formulas and explained how haste would lend
conviction. He bowed to Gathon. "Lord Voice, you have heard
how we were borne from our different countries. We did not
know if this was by an accident of sorcery, or the caprice of a
Being, or a divine will. In the last case, Whose, and what is
required of us?

"Today we went forth, looking for a secluded place where we
might talk. The king's man who guided us suggested the Grove
of Periboea. There the lady Erissa made oblation according to
the Keftiu rite of the Goddess she serves. Presently a sleep came
upon us that lasted for hours, and a dream. Awakening, we
found we had all had the same dream—yes, even our guide."

Oleg shifted his stance, folded and unfolded his arms. He had
watched Erissa plant that vision in Peneleos. Uldin sneered
faintly, or was it a trick of the light wavering over his scars? A
gust of rain blew down the smokehole; the hearthfire sputtered,
steamed, and coughed forth gray billows.

Gathon signed himself. However, his gaze, resting on Reid,
showed probing intelligence rather than the unease which
alloyed Aegeus' pain and exhaustion, Theseus' throttled fury,
Diores' poised alertness. "Surely this is the work of a Being,"
he said levelly. "What was the dream?"

"As we have told my lords here," Reid answered, "a woman
came, dressed like a high-born Keftiu lady. We did not see her

face, or else we cannot recall it. In either hand she carried a snake that twined back along the arm. She said, whispering rather than speaking, so that her tone became one with the hissing of the snakes: 'Only strangers out of strangeness have power to carry this word, that houses sundered shall be bound together and the sea shall be pierced and made fruitful by the lightning in that hour when the Bull shall wed the Owl; but woe betide if they hear not!'"

There followed a stillness within the storm. In an age when everyone believed the gods or the dead spoke prophecies to men, none were surprised that a revelation had come to these who were already charged with fate. But the meaning must be anxiously sought.

Reid and Erissa hadn't dared be more explicit. Oracles weren't. Diores would probably have accused them of lying if his man hadn't backed them; and he might well be skeptical regardless.

"How would you read this, Voice?" Theseus asked.

"What do those think who were given it?" the Minoan responded.

"We believe we are commanded to go to your country," Reid stated. "In fact—no disrespect to our hosts—we think ourselves bound to offer what service we can to him who is their sovereign."

"Had the gods intended that," Theseus said, "they could better have sent a Cretan ship to Egypt for you."

"But then the strangers would never have come to Athens," Gathon pointed out. "And the message does sound as if somehow they're destined to . . . bring sundered houses together. . . . Ill will has flourished between our countries, and the passage of time has not much bettered things. These men come from so far away that their motives are less suspect than might otherwise be the case. Hence they may be the go-betweens who make it possible that the will of the gods be done. If the Bull of Keft shall wed the Owl of Athens—if the lightning of Zeus shall make fruitful the waters of Our Lady—that suggests an alliance. Perhaps a royal marriage between Labyrinth and Acropolis, from which a most glorious king will be born? Yes, these people must certainly go to Knossos for further talks. At once. The season's not too advanced for a good ship and crew to take them."

Abruptly Uldin snapped, "I think not!"

You son of a bitch, flashed through Reid.

His anger died. The Hun knew they were faking, knew they were trying to reach a land whose downfall was prophesied. He had argued bitterly in the grove that to take the losing side—a race of sailors at that!—was lunatic enough, but to add blasphemy suggested demonic possession. He had only been won over to the extent of pledging silence when Reid explained about contact with Atlantis being essential to winning home. Now his fears must have convinced him that that chance wasn't worth the risk.

Oleg glowered at him. "Why not?"

"I—well—" Uldin straightened. "Well, I promised Diores I'd undertake certain matters. Do the gods want broken promises?"

"Do we indeed know what their will is?" Theseus put in. "The oracle could mean the very opposite of what my lord Voice suggests. A warning of disaster if, once more, an unnatural union is made." The teeth flashed in his beard.

Gathon stiffened at the hardly veiled reference to a dirty story the Achaeans told about how the first Minotaur was begotten. "My sovereign will not be pleased if he learns that a word intended for him has been withheld like a pair of helmets," he said.

Impasse. Neither side wanted the other to have the castaways, their possibly revolutionary skills and their surely enormous *mana*. Nor did either want an open quarrel, yet.

Diores stepped forward. He raised his arm. A smile creased his leathery visage. "My lords," he said. "My friends. Will you hear me?" The prince nodded. "I'm just an old skipper and horse-breeder," Diores continued. "I don't have your wise heads nor your deep learning. Still, sometimes a clever man stands by the steering oar trying to figure out what's ahead of him and gets nowhere till his dolt of a shipmate swarms up the mast and takes a look. Right?"

He beamed and gestured, playing to his audience. "Well, now," he drawled through seething rain, yammering wind, spitting flames, "what have we got here? On the one hand, we have that the gods have naught against these good folk dwelling amongst us Athenians, seeing as how nothing bad has happened because of that. Right? On the other hand, we have that the Minos is entitled to see them too—if it's not dangerous—and we think maybe the gods gave 'em their sailing orders today. We *think*." He laid a finger alongside his nose. "Do we *know*? These be shoal waters, mates, and a lee shore. I say row slow and take soundings . . . also for the sake of the Keftiu, Voice Gathon."

"What do you propose?" the Cretan asked impatiently.

"Why, I'll say it straight out, like a blunt-spoken old wooden-head does. Let's first learn what those think who know more about the gods, and especial-like the Keftiu gods, than we do here. I mean the Ariadne and her council on Atlantis—"

Theseus sat bolt upright. His hand cracked down on his knee. The breath rushed between his lips. Reid wondered why he was thus immediately kindled to enthusiasm.

"—and I mean further that we shouldn't risk sending the lot of 'em, the more so when stormy season is on us. Why not just one who'll speak for his friends, which friends I hope include everybody here tonight? And—m-m-m, wouldn't y' say Duncan would be best to go? I mean, he's the wisest of 'em, no offense to Uldin and Oleg. Nor to lady Erissa when she hears about my remarks. Thing is, she don't know anything the Ariadne don't. But Duncan comes from the farthest country; he was the man who could understand what the dying wizard had to tell; he can make fire spurt in his fingers; I don't know what all else, except that they look to him for advice about mysteries, and rightly, I'm sure. Let him go talk to the Ariadne on Atlantis. Between 'em they're bound to heave clear this fouled anchor we've got. Right?"

"Right, by Ares!" Theseus exploded.

Gathon nodded thoughtfully. He could doubtless see the plan was a compromise which allowed the Athenians to keep hostages and exploit their knowledge, more useful than Reid's. However, this was a portentous, ambiguous affair; caution was advisable; and the Ariadne did have the Keftiu in her spiritual keeping.

This is what was foreordained, Reid knew. The sense of fate took him again, as it had done beneath the moon on Kythera; but now it felt as if he were a raindrop hurled along on the night wind.

They left a lamp burning. The glow caressed Erissa like his hand. "Does it make me look young?" she whispered through tears.

Reid kissed her lips and the hollow beneath her throat. She was warm in the cold room. Her muscles moved silkily across his skin where they touched each other on the bed; the odor of her was sweet as the meadow of the nymph. "You're beautiful" was the single poor thing he could find to say.

"Already tomorrow—"

A day had passed in preparing for the voyage. He and she had spent it together, and the hell with what anybody thought.

"We dare not wait, this time of year."

"I know, I know. Though you could. You can't be wrecked, Duncan. You'll come safe to Atlantis. You did." She buried her face against his shoulder. He felt the wetness of it. Her hair spilled across his breast. "Am I trying to cheat that girl out of a few days? Yes. But no use, is it? Oh, how glad I am we know nothing about what happens to us after next springtime! I couldn't bear that."

"I believe you could bear anything, Erissa."

She lay breathing awhile. Finally, raising herself over him and looking down, she said: "Well, it need not be utter doom. Why, we may even save my people. We may be the blade the gods use to trim back a destiny that grew crooked. Will you strive where you are, Duncan, as I'll strive here while I wait for you?"

"Yes," he promised, and in this hour, at least, he was honest.

Not that he believed they could rescue her world. Or if they were able to—if human will could really turn the stars in their courses—for to change what had been would be to change the universe out to its last year and light-year—he would never condemn Bitsy to having never been born. Yet might he not imaginably find a door left open in this cage of time?

Erissa fought to achieve a smile, and won. "Then let's mourn no longer," she said. "Love me till dawn."

He had not known what loving could be, before her.

# TWELVE

THE EERINESS of the fate that waited for him could not take from Reid all his wonder at coming to lost Atlantis.

It rose from a sea which today was more green than blue, whitecaps running like the small swift clouds above. Approximately circular, a trifle over eleven miles across, the island climbed in rugged tiers from its coasts. Where cliff or crag stood bare, the stone showed blacks, dull reds, and startling pale pumice below. From the middle, the cone of the mountain loomed in naked lava and cinders. A trail could be seen winding up to the still quiescent crater. A lesser volcano thrust from the waves not far offshore.

At first view the overlay of life was unspectacular. The word that crossed Reid's mind was "charming." Fields, autumnally ocher, were tucked into pockets of soil; but most agriculture was orchards, olive, fig, apple, or vineyards which now glowed red and purple. Still more of the steep land was left in grass, pungent shrubs, scattered oak or cypress made into bonsai by thin earth and salt winds. Reid was surprised to see that it pastured not the elsewhere omnipresent goats, but large red-and-white cattle; then he remembered that this was the holy place of the Keftiu and Erissa (today, today!) danced with those huge-horned bulls.

Farmsteads lay well apart. Their houses were similar to those in Greece or throughout the Mediterranean countries, squarish flat-roofed adobes. Many had exterior staircases, but few windows faced outward; a home surrounded a courtyard whereon the family's existence was centered. However, the Keftiu were distinctive in their use of pastel stucco and vivid mural patterns.

Fisher boats were busy across the waters; otherwise no vessels moved except Diores'. A cloud mass on the southern horizon betokened Crete.

Reid drew his cloak tighter about him against the chill. Was Atlantis no more than this?

The ship rowed past a lesser island which, between abrupt cliffs, guarded the mouth of a miles-wide lagoon. Reid saw that the great volcano stood in the middle of that bay. He saw, too, that here was indeed a place legend would never forget.

Off the starboard bow, a city covered the hills that rose from the water. It was at least as big as Athens, more carefully laid out, delightful to the eye in its manifold colors, and it needed no wall for defense. Its docks were mostly vacant, the majority of ships drawn ashore for winter. Reid noticed several hulls being scraped and painted on an artificially widened beach some distance further off; others were already at rest in the sheds behind. A couple of warcraft, fishtailed and eagle-prowed, were moored at readiness, reminders of the sea king's might.

Here in the sheltering heart of the island, water sparkled blue and quiet, the air was warm and the breezes soft. A number of small boats cruised around under sail. Their gay trim, the women and children among their passengers, marked them as pleasure craft.

Diores pointed to the gatewarden isle. "Yonder's where we'll go," he said. "But first we tie up at town and get leave to come see the Ariadne."

Reid nodded. You wouldn't let just anybody onto your sanctum. The isle was superbly landscaped; terraces bore gardens which had yet some flowerbeds to vie with arbors turning bronze and gold. On its crest spread a complex of buildings, only two stories high but impressively wide, made from cyclopean blocks of stone. These were painted white, and across that background went a mural frieze: humans, bulls, octopuses, peacocks, monkeys, chimeras, a procession dancing from either side of the main gate to the pillars which flanked it. They were bright red, those pillars; Erissa had told Reid the column was a sacred symbol. Another sign was inset in gold over the lintel: the double ax, the Labrys. The third emblem curved on the roof above, a pair of great gilded horns.

"Will we have a long wait?" he asked. A part of him marveled rather sadly at how, no matter what adventure or what contortions of destiny, most time got eaten up by ordinariness. However taciturn his forebodings had made him on the voyage here, he had not been spared hours of prosaic chatter. (And no serious talk. Diores had skillfully avoided letting that develop.)

"Not us," the Athenian said, "after she hears we're from Prince Theseus."

That mention of heir rather than king hauled Reid's attention to the sharp gray-bearded face before him. "Are they close friends, then?" he flung out.

Diores squirted a stream of saliva leisurely over the side. "Well," he said when he had finished, "they've met now and again. You know how the prince has traveled about. Naturally he'd look in on the Ariadne. Be rude not to, wouldn't it? And she's less of a snob about us Achaeans than you might look for, which could be helpful. Got a bit of Kalydonian blood in her, in fact, though born in Knossos. Ye-e-es, I expect we'll be well received."

The unseasonal arrival of a ship drew a crowd to the wharf. They were a carefree lot. Teeth flashed in bronzed faces, hands flew in gestures, words and laughter spilled forth. There was no evidence of poverty; Atlantis must wax rich off the pilgrimage trade as well as its mundane industries; yet the Greeks had spoken to Reid, with considerable envy, about a similar prosperity throughout the realm of the Minos.

Of course, by the standards of Reid's milieu, even the well-to-do here lived austerely. But how much genuine well-being lay in a glut of gadgets? Given a fertile sea in a gentle climate, surrounded by natural beauty, free of war or the threat of it, who needed more?

When the Minoan worked, he worked hard, often dangerously. But his basic needs were soon taken care of; the government, drawing its income from tariffs, tribute, and royal properties, made no demands on him; how much extra toil he put in depended on how big a share of available luxuries he desired. He always left himself ample time for loafing, swimming, sport fishing, partying, lovemaking, worship, joy. Reid had gotten the distinct impression that Keftiu, 1400 B.C., had more leisure and probably more individual liberty than Americans, 1970 A.D.

The harbormaster resembled Gathon but wore typically Cretan garb: a tightly wound white loincloth which doubled as padding for a bronze girdle; boots and puttees; wraparound headgear; jewelry at neck, wrists, and ankles. He carried a staff of office topped with the double ax, and a peacock plume in his turban. His fellow males were clad likewise, though less elaborately. Most went bareheaded, some had a small cap, some chose shoes or sandals or nothing on the feet, the loincloths might be in gaudy patterns, the belts were oftener leather than metal. Both sexes wore those cinctures; they could be seen around otherwise naked children, constricting the waist to that narrowness admired by the Keftiu; only the elderly gave their bellies room to relax.

Diores nudged Reid. "I must admit, mate, Cretish girls put on a brave show," he leered. "Eh? And it's not hard finding a wench who'll tumble, either, after a bit o' fast talk, maybe a stoup o' wine or a bauble. I wouldn't let my daughters run loose like that, but it does make fun for a sailorman, right?"

Most women were dressed merely in ankle-length skirts; they were commoners, bearing groceries or laundry or water jugs or babies. But some more fashionable types had crinolines elaborately flounced; and embroidered bodices, with or without a gauzy chemise, that upheld but did not cover the breasts; and stone-studded copper, tin, bronze, silver, gold, amber ornamentation; and saucy little sandals; and as wide a variety of hats as ever along Reid's Champs Elysées; and makeup of talc and rouge for more areas than the face. When the Achaean crew shouted lusty greetings, the younger girls were apt to giggle and wave handkerchiefs in reply.

Diores and Reid explained to the harbormaster that they had official business with the Ariadne. He bowed. "Of course, sirs," he said. "I'll dispatch a courier boat at once, and you'll doubtless be received tomorrow morning." He rested a bright glance on Reid, obviously curious as to what manner of foreigner this might be. "Meanwhile, will you not honor my house?"

"I thank you," Reid said. Diores was less pleased, having looked forward to a rowdy evening in a waterfront inn, but was forced to accept too.

The streets lacked sidewalks; closely packed buildings hemmed them in between walls or booths. But they were wide, reasonably straight, paved with well-dressed stone. A market square displayed a stunning mosaic of octopus and lilies; at its center splashed a fountain, where children played under the eyes of mothers or nurses. The outdoor cleanliness was due to a sophisticated drainage and refuse disposal system. The workaday bustle recalled that of Athens but was somehow more orderly, easygoing, and happy. And it included sights unknown among those Achaeans who had not adopted Cretan civilization—shops offering wares from as far as Britain, Spain, Ethiopia, or India; public scribes; an architect sketching on papyrus his rendering of a proposed house; a school letting out, boys and girls together carrying styluses and waxed tablets for their homework and not appearing to be exclusively children of the rich, either; a blind lyrist playing and singing, his bowl at his feet for donations of food—

*"Like rainstorms on an autumn sea,*
*Sun-stabbed by spears of brazen light,*
*Your whirlwind love nigh capsized me.*
*Like rainstorms on an autumn sea,*
*You've left a gentle memory.*
*Come back and whip the billows white*
*Like rainstorms on an autumn sea,*
*Sun-stabbed by spears of brazen light!"*

The harbormaster's house was large enough to require two patios for ventilation. Its rooms were decorated with frescos of animals, plants, waves in the lively and naturalistic Cretan style. Floors were pebbled cement covered by mats; you removed footgear before entering. Pamela would have admired the furniture: wooden chests, bedsteads, and chairs; round-topped stone tables; lamps, jars, braziers of different sizes and shapes. The workmanship was exquisite, the colors pleasing. A niche held a terracotta image of the Goddess in Her aspect of Rhea the Mother. The entire family washed themselves, knelt, and asked Her blessing before dinner.

After Aegeus' board, Reid rejoiced in well-prepared seafood, vegetables, wheat bread, goat cheese, honeycake for dessert, an excellent wine. The conversation was that of a civilized host, especially interested in astronomy and natural history, who didn't mind letting his wife and their offspring join in. No one got drunk and no slave girls waited in the guest chambers. (In fact, while slaves were common elsewhere in the Thalassocracy, they were forbidden to be brought to holy Atlantis. There a servant was usually the daughter of poor parents, paid in food, lodging, and an eventual dowry.)

Lying in a bed too small, Reid wondered how the Keftiu,

preservers of law and peace, carriers of a trade that brought prosperity to every realm it touched, clean, friendly, mannerly, learned, gifted, totally human, would come to be remembered for a man-devouring monster in horrible corridors. Well, he thought, the victors write the chronicles, eventually the legends.

He opened his eyes. For the sake of fresh air, he'd left the door to the adjoining courtyard open. The night was clear, murmurous, frosted with stars. But up across them reared the black mass of the volcano; and it had begun to smoke.

Lydra, the Ariadne of Atlantis, touched Reid's brow. "In the name of the Goddess and Asterion, blessings." Her formal words were flattened out by the wariness that looked from her eyes.

He bowed. "Forgive an outlander, my lady, if he does not know what is proper behavior," he said awkwardly.

Silence fell and continued in that long dim room. At its southern end, the door giving on a light-well was closed against rain. Opposite gaped darkness, a hallway leading deeper into the maze of the palace-temple. A mural on the south side showed Her three aspects together, Maiden, Mother, and Hag. On the north side, human figures who had the heads and wings of eagles escorted the dead to judgment. The pictures had all the Cretan realism, none of the Cretan joyfulness. By flickering lamplight, they seemed to stir. Smoke from bronze braziers curled before them, sweetened by sandalwood but stinging nostrils in this bleak air.

"Well." The high priestess sought her cushioned marble throne. "Be seated if you wish."

Reid took a stool beneath her. What next? he wondered. Yesterday he and Diores had been received with ritual courtesy. Afterward a pair of consecrates gave the American a guided tour of the publicly showable areas while the Athenian and the Ariadne were closeted alone for hours. That evening, back at the harbormaster's house, Diores was evasive: "—Oh, she wanted the gossip from our parts. And I had orders to ask about getting the Temple's help toward liberalizing the treaty—like letting us keep more warcraft for protecting our interests in the Euxine where the Cretans don't patrol—you know. She'll see you private tomorrow. Now have another cupful, if our host'll be that kind, and simmer down."

Reid studied her as carefully as he dared. Lydra was in her later thirties, he'd been told: tall, stiffly erect, slender on the verge of gauntness. Her face, likewise lean, bore blue-gray eyes, arching nose, severely held mouth, strong chin. The brown hair had started to fade, the breasts to sag, though she kept part of the bull dancer physique from her youth. She wore the full farthingale, the high brimless hat, the golden snake bracelets seen upon images of Rhea. A blue cloak was thrown over her shoulders. Reid felt like a barbarian in his Achaean tunic and beard.

Or was his unease because he distrusted her? He'd found a chance to tell Erissa: "A story persisted to my day that . . . an Ariadne . . . helped Theseus slay the Minotaur. What could be the truth behind it?"

Erissa had shrugged. "I heard—will hear—rumors that he and she were in conspiracy. But the only clear fact is that after the disaster she joined him in conducting sacrifice, and later she departed in his ship. Well, what choice had she? He needed her to cast some thin legitimacy over his conquest of Knossos, and had the strength to compel her. She never reached Athens. He left her and her attendants on the island of Naxos. There, despairing, they gave up the pure faith and turned to a mystery cult. If anything, does such treatment not show that no bargain existed, that she was—is, will be—innocent?"

"But, well, I hear Theseus has been on Atlantis more than once, and messages often travel back and forth."

Erissa had uttered a sad small laugh. "Why should he not cultivate the spiritual head of the Thalassocracy? She did have a Kalydonian grandfather. But fear not her ever serving in earnest a worldly cause. Her maidenhead was scarcely fledged when she had a revelation in the cave of Mount Iouktas. Since, she's always called herself a bride of Asterion. After her bull dancing days, she took the vows of a priestess—among them celibacy, remember—and served so devotedly that she was elected to regnancy over the Temple at the lowest age on record. I well recall her austerities, her strict enforcement of every observance, her lectures to us lay sisters about our vanities, levities, and laxities." Seriously: "What you must do is convince her you are an agent of good, not evil; and that may not be easy, Duncan, darling."

Right, he now thought, gazing into the implacable countenance.

"These are grave matters, touching on secrets that the gods withhold from mortals," Lydra said. "And I do not mean things like your fire-spouter, or the iron and the horse riding that Diores spoke of. Those are simply human works. The moon-disk you bear on your arm, however—"

He had demonstrated his wristwatch yesterday and noticed how awed the attendant votaresses were. Though folk used sun and stars to mark off units as small as hours, these blades which busily scissored away each successive instant were too reminding of Dictynna the Gatherer.

He saw an opportunity. "Besides a timepiece, my lady, it's an amulet which confers certain prophetic powers. I'd planned on giving it to the Minos, but maybe the proper repository is here." He took it off and laid it in her hand, which closed almost convulsively around it. "The oracle did not come to us outlanders by chance. I can foresee terrible dangers. My mission is to warn your people. I dared not tell the Athenians."

Lydra set the watch down and touched the Labrys talisman to her lips. "What do you mean?" she asked tonelessly.

Here we go, Reid thought, and wondered if he was about to destroy the world he had come from, like summer sunlight scorching a morning mist off the earth; or if he was only fluttering his wings in the cage of time.

Neither, I hope, I pray my agnostic prayer, he thought amidst the knockings of his heart. I hope to gain the influence I must have in order to do . . . whatever is needful . . . to find those travelers from the future when they come, and thus win home to my wife and children. In exchange, can I not salvage a little of Erissa's world for her? Or at least get her back to the one she salvaged for herself?

It is my duty. I suppose it is also my desire.

"My lady," he said solemnly, out of a dry mouth, "I have been shown visions of horror, visions of doom. I have been shown Pillar Mountain bursting asunder in such fury that Atlantis sinks beneath the sea, tidal waves overwhelm the fleet and earthquakes the cities of Crete, and the royal island falls prey to men who set chaos free to roam."

He might have gone on to what he remembered from books not yet written: A sleazy reconstruction under the new rulers, who must surely be Achaeans and who had no wish to keep the peace either at sea or on land. The Homeric era to follow; would splendid lines of poetry really repay lifetimes of disintegration, war, piracy, banditry, rape, slaughter, burning, poverty, and glutted slave markets? Finally, that invasion from the north which Theseus himself was troubled about: wild Dorians bearing iron weapons, bringing the Bronze Age down in ruin so total that scarcely a legend would remain of the dark centuries which came after.

Lydra, who had sat still a while, spoke. "When is this to happen?"

"Early next year, my lady. If preparations can be made—"

"Wait. A fumbling attempt at rescue could be the very cause of disaster. The gods have been known to work deviously when they would destroy."

"My lady, I speak only of evacuating the Atlanteans to Crete and everyone there inland from the coastal towns . . . safeguarding the fleet—"

The pale eyes held most steady upon him. "You could have been misled," she told him slowly, "whether by a hostile Being or an evil-seeking witch or a mere fever. You could even be lying for some purpose of your own."

"You must have had a full report on me from Diores, my lady."

"Not full enough, obviously." Lydra raised a hand. "Hold. I make no accusation against you. Indeed, what I have heard, what I see in your expression, makes me think you're likely honest—as far as you go—but you do not go very far, do you, strange one? No, something this drastic requires askings out, purifications, prayers, visits to oracles, takings of counsel, the deepest search and pondering that mortals can make. I will not be hastened. According to your own word, we have months before us wherein to seek the wisest course of action."

Decisive as any man he had known, she finished: "You will stay on this isle, where sacredness holds bane at bay and where you can readily be summoned for further talks. There are ample guest quarters in the wing reserved for visiting male votaries."

"But my lady," he protested, "my friends in Athens—"

"Let them bide where they are, at least until we've learned more. Be not afraid for them. Winter months or no, I'll find occasions to send messengers there, who'll observe and report."

The Ariadne imitated a smile. "You are not a prisoner, man from afar," she continued. "You may walk freely about the main island too, when not needed here. I do want you always under guidance. . . . Let me think. . . . A dancer should suffice, a lay sister, young and merry to brighten your moods."

Reid thought it odd how calmly she took his news. Had Diores ferreted out sufficient hints to give her forewarning, or was she inhumanly self-controlled? Her voice snapped the thread of his wondering:

"I have in mind particularly a sister of excellent family whose name may be an omen. For it's the same as that of your woman companion I was told about. Erissa."

# THIRTEEN

THE BULL lowered his head, pawed, and charged. As he came down the paddock he gathered speed, until earth shook and drummed with the red-and-white mass of him.

Poised, the girl waited. She was clad like a boy for this, in nothing more than belt, kilt, and soft boots. Dark hair fell down her back in a ponytail lest a stray lock blind her. Reid's nails dug into his palms.

Sunlight out of a wan sky flashed off tridents borne by the men on guard. In an emergency, they were supposed to rescue the dancers. They stood at ease just outside the rail fence. Reid couldn't. Through the cool breeze, the hay and marjoram odors of Atlantis' high meadows, he sensed his own sweat trickling, stinking, catching in his mustache and making his lips taste salty when he wet them.

That was Erissa waiting for those horns.

But she won't be hurt, he told himself frantically. Not yet.

At his back the hills rolled downward, yellow grass, green bush, here and there a copse of gnarly trees, to a remote glimmer off the sea. Before him was the training field, and beyond that a slope more abrupt, and at its foot the city, the bay, the sacred isle, and that other isle which, rising black from scintillant blueness, was the volcano. Above the crater stood a column of smoke so thick that the wind hardly bent its first thousand feet. Higher up it was scattered and blown south toward unseen Knossos.

The bull was almost upon the girl. Behind her a half-dozen companions wove a quick-footed pattern of dance.

Erissa sprang. Either hand seized a horn. The muscles played beneath her skin. Incredibly to Reid, she lifted herself, waved legs aloft, before she let go—and somersaulted down the great backbone, reached ground in an exuberant flip, and pranced her way back into the group. Another slender form was already on the horns.

"She's good, that 'un." A guard nodded at Erissa, winked at Reid. "But she'll take no priestess vows, I'll bet. The man who beds her 'ull have as much as he can handle— Hoy!" He leaped onto a rail, ready to jump the fence with his fellows. The bull had bellowed and tossed his head, flinging a girl aside.

Erissa ran to the beast, tugged an ear, and pirouetted off. He swerved toward her. She repeated her vault over him. The dance resumed, the guards relaxed.

"Thought for a bit there he was turning mean," said the man who had earlier spoken. "But he just got excited. Happens."

Reid let out a breath. His knees were about to give way. "Do . . . you lose . . . many people?" he whispered.

"No, very seldom, and those who're gored often recover. That's here on Atlantis, I mean. The boys train on Crete, and I'm told no few of them get hurt. Boys're too reckless. They're more interested in making a good show, winning glory for themselves, than in honoring the gods. Girls, now, girls want the rite to go perfect for Her, so they pay close attention and follow the rules."

The bull, which had been rushing at each one who separated herself from the group, slowed to a walk, then stopped. His flanks gleamed damp and his breath was loud. "That'll do," the ringmaster decided, waved his trident and shouted, "Everybody out!" To Reid he explained, "The nasty incidents are usually when the beast's gotten tired. He doesn't want to play any more, and if you force him, he's apt to lose his temper. Or he may simply forget what he's supposed to do."

The girls scampered over the fence. The bull snorted. "Leave him a while to cool off before you open the gate," the ringmaster said. He cast a glance more appraising than appreciative over the bare young breasts and limbs, wet as the animal's. "Enough for today, youngsters. Put your cloaks on so you don't catch cold and go to the boat."

They obeyed and departed, chattering and giggling like any lot of twelve- and thirteen-year-olds. They were no more than that, new recruits learning the art. The bull, however, was a veteran. You didn't exercise together humans and beasts when neither knew what to expect.

And that, Reid thought, is the secret of the Minoan corrida. Nobody in my era, that I read about anyway, could figure out how it was possible. The answer looks obvious, now. You breed your cattle, not for slowness as Mary Renault suggested, but for intelligence; and you train them from calfhood.

Nonetheless it's dangerous. A misstep, a flareup . . . They don't accept every kid who wants fame and prizes and influence. No; bloodshed's a bad omen. (Except the blood of the best animal, when he's sacrificed after the games.) That must be the reason—beneath every religious rationalization—why the maidens aren't allowed to dance when they're having a period and why they have to stay maidens. Morning sickness would raise hell with an agility and coordination that would earn them black belts in any judo school at home, wouldn't it? And there, in turn, we must have the reason why they train here, the youths on Crete. Put together a mixed lot of young, good-looking, physically perfect human beings—

Erissa neared. "Well," she smiled, "did you enjoy watching?"

"It was, was unique in my life," he stammered.

She halted before him. So far she had only flung her cloak across an arm. The ringmaster's orders did not touch her, who, with long experience, had been the instructress. "I don't want to go back to the isle right away," she said. "The men can take the girls. You and I can borrow a shallop later." She drew the crow's-wing queue off her bosom where it had gotten tossed. "After all, the Ariadne told me to show you about."

"You are too kind."

"No, you are interesting." He could not draw his eyes from her. Erissa—seventeen years old, colt slim, unscarred by time or grief, loosening her hair . . . Her smile faded. A slow flush descended from cheeks to breasts. She flung the wool cloak over her shoulders and pulled it around her. "Why do you stare?"

"I'm sorry," Reid mumbled. "You're, uh, the first real bull dancer I've met."

"Oh." She relaxed. "I'm nothing remarkable. Wait till we go to Knossos in spring and you see the festival." She pinned her mantle at the throat. "Shall we walk?"

He fell into step beside her. "Do you live here throughout every winter?" he asked, knowing the answer from her older self but feeling a need of staving off silence.

"Yes, to help train novices, and beasts, and myself after a summer's ease. That's spent in Knossos, mostly, or in a country villa we have. Sometimes we go elsewhere, though. My father's a wealthy man, he owns several ships, and he'll give us, his children, passage when a voyage is to a pleasant place."

"M-m, how did he feel when you wanted to become a dancer?"

"I had to wheedle him a little. Mother made the real fuss. Not that parents can stop you from trying out. But I didn't want to hurt them. I hadn't gotten a real call, like the one that came to Ariadne Lydra. It just seemed exciting, glamorous—am I shocking you? Please don't think I'm not happy to serve Our Lady and Asterion. But I wouldn't want to become a priestess. I want lots of children. And, you know, a dancer meets practically every eligible bachelor in the Thalassocracy. With the honor she'll bring to his house, she can pretty well choose any of them. Maybe this spring will be my last festival to dance in—" Her trilling stopped. She caught his hand. "Why, Duncan, your mouth is all twisted up. You look ready to weep. What's wrong?"

"Nothing," he said harshly. "I remembered an old hurt."

She continued hand in hand with him. No man on Atlantis would dare take advantage of her, he thought. The paddock was lost to view as their trail wound downward over the hills. Grass and brush stirred, trees soughed in the wind. He could smell her flesh, still warm from exertion, warm as the sunlight on his back or the fingers that curled around his.

"Tell me of yourself," she urged presently. "You must be very important for the Ariadne to keep you."

Lydra had commanded strict silence about his prediction of catastrophe. He had to admit that, for the time being, it made sense; public hysteria would help nothing. She'd wanted to suppress the entire story of his magical arrival in Egypt, but he pointed out that that was impossible. The word had spread through Athens and Diores' sailors must have passed it around Atlantean taverns and bawdyhouses before returning home.

"I don't know that I myself count for much," Reid said to the girl. "But I've come a far and a weird way and am hoping the high priestess can counsel me."

He gave her simply his public narrative, no hint about time travel but much about America. She listened wide-eyed. As he talked, he tried to recall Pamela's face. But he couldn't, really, for Erissa's—young Erissa's.

Lydra said: "You will remain here until I release you."

"I tell you, the Minos must be warned," Reid protested.

"Will my word carry less weight with him than yours?" she retorted coldly. "I am still not satisfied you speak truth, exile."

No, he thought, I don't imagine any rational person is ever ready to believe in the end of his world.

They stood on the temple roof in a chilly dusk. The lagoon glimmered faintly metallic; land and city were swallowed by murk, in this age before outdoor lighting. But fire was in the sky, a sullen red flicker reflected off the smoke that rolled out of the volcano. Now and then sparks showered from its throat and there went an underground rumbling.

He gestured. "Does that not bear witness for me?"

"It has spoken before," she answered. "Sometimes it spews forth stones and cinders and melted rock, and the voice of Asterion roars. But a procession to the heights, prayers, sacrifices cast in, have always quieted him. Would he destroy the sanctuary of his Mother, his Bride, and his Mourner?"

Reid threw her a glance. Beneath a cowl, her profile showed vague against darkling heaven; but he made out that she was staring at the mountain more intently than her calm tone suggested. "You can smooth the people's unease," he said, "till the last day. What about your own, though?"

"I am praying for guidance."

"What harm in sending me to Knossos?"

"What good, thus far? Hear me, outlander. I reign over holy things, not over men. But this does not mean I'm ignorant of temporal affairs. I could hardly be that and serve Our Lady's interests. So I understand, perhaps better than you if you are honest about your origin—I understand how grave a matter it would be to follow your advice.

"Cities emptied, left deserted . . . for weeks? Think of moving that many people, feeding and sheltering them, keeping them from blind panic at the awful thing threatened, losing them by hundreds or thousands when sickness breaks out in their camps, as it surely will. And meanwhile the navy is far at sea, widely scattered for fear ships will be dashed together, therefore helpless. But boats would speedily carry news to the mainland. The risk that the Achaeans would revolt again, make alliance and fall on our coasts, is not small. And *then*, if your prophecy proved false—what anger throughout the realm, what mockery of temple and throne and the very gods—what rebellion, even, shaking the already cracked foundations of the state! No, that which you urge is not lightly to be undertaken."

Reid grimaced. She spoke with reason. "That's why plans have to be laid soon," he begged. "What can I do to prove myself to you?"

"Have you a suggestion?"

"Well—" The idea had come to him already in Athens. He and Oleg had discussed it at length. "Yes. If you, my lady, can persuade the temporal governor—wh-wh-which you surely can—"

The mountain growled again.

Sarpedon, master of Atlantis' one small shipyard, ran a hand through his thinning gray hair. "I'm doubtful," he said. "We're not set up here like at Knossos or Tiryns, you know. We mainly do repair and maintenance work. Don't actually build anything larger than a boat." He stared down at the papyrus Reid had spread on a table. A finger traced the drawing. "Still—but no. Too much material needed."

"The governor will release timber, bronze, cordage, everything, from the royal warehouse," Reid pressed him. "He only asks for your agreement on feasibility. And it is feasible. I've seen craft like this in action."

That wasn't true, unless you counted movies. (A world of moving pictures, light at the flick of a switch, motors, skyscrapers, spacecraft, antibiotics, radio links, an hour's hop through the air between Crete and Athens . . . unreal, fantastic, a fading dream. Reality was this cluttered room, this man who wore a loincloth and worshipped a bull that was also the sun, the creak of wooden wheels and the clop-clop of unshod donkey hoofs from a street outside, a street in lost Atlantis; reality was the girl who held his arm and waited breathlessly for him to unfold his next marvel.) But he had read books; and, while he was not a marine designer, as an architect he was necessarily enough of an engineer for this work.

"Um-m. Um-m." Sarpedon tugged his chin. "Fascinating notion, I must say."

"I don't understand what difference it will make," Erissa ventured shyly. "I'm sorry, but I don't."

"At present," Reid explained, "a ship is nothing but a means for getting from here to there."

She blinked. Her lashes were longer and thicker, her eyes even more luminous, than they would be when she was forty and fading. "Oh, but ships are beautiful!" she said. "And sacred to Our Lady of the Deeps." The second sentence was dutiful; the first shone from her.

"Well, in war, then." Reid sighed. "Consider. Except for slingstones, arrows, and javelins, you can't have a real battle at sea before you've grappled fast to your enemy. And then it's a matter of boarding, hand-to-hand combat, no different from a fight on land except that quarters are cramped and footing uncertain."

He returned his glance to Sarpedon, reluctantly. "I admit that a vessel such as I propose will use more stuff than a regular galley," he told the yardmaster. "In particular, it'll tie up a great deal of bronze in its beak. However, the strength of Crete has always lain in keels rather than spears, right? Whatever makes a more effective navy will repay the Thalassocrat ten times over.

"Now." He tapped his drawing. "The ram alone is irresistible. You know how fragile hulls are. This prow is reinforced. Striking, it'll send any opponent to the bottom. Soldiers aren't needed, just sailors. Think of the saving in manpower. And because this vessel can destroy one after another in a full-dress naval engagement, fewer of its type are needed than galleys. So the size of the navy can be reduced. You get a large net saving in materials too."

Erissa looked distressed. "But we have no enemies left," she said.

The hell you don't, Reid didn't say. Instead: "Well, you mount guard against possible preparation for hostilities. And you maintain patrols to suppress piracy. And those same patrols give aid to distressed vessels, which is good for commerce and so for your prosperity. And there are no few voyages to waters where the Minos does not rule and the natives might get greedy. True?

"Very well. This longer hull gives greater speed. And this strange-looking rudder and rig make it possible to sail against any but the foulest winds, crisscrossing them. Oarsmen tire and need rest oftener than airs drop to a dead calm. What we have here is a ship that's not only invincible but can out-travel anything you've ever imagined. Therefore, again, fewer are required for any given purpose. The savings can go into making the realm stronger and wealthier.

"The governor is most interested," Reid finished pointedly, "and likewise the Ariadne."

"Well, I'm interested too," Sarpedon replied. "I'd like to try it. By Asterion's tail, I would—! Um, beg pardon, Sister. . . . But I dare not pledge it'll succeed. The work'd go slowly at best. Not only because we've no large facilities here. You wouldn't believe how conservative shipwrights, carpenters, sailmakers, the whole lot of them are. We'd have to stand over them with cudgels, I swear, to make them turn out work as peculiar as this." Shrewdly: "And no doubt we'll have many a botch, many a detail nobody had thought of. And sailors are at least as hidebound as craftsmen. You'll not get them to learn a whole new way of seafaring. Better you recruit among young fellows itchy for adventure. The town'll have ample of those, now when winter's closing down the trade lanes. However, training them up will take time also."

"I have time," Reid snapped.

Lydra was not about to let him go. And she might well be right, that some such proof of his bona fides as this was needful. Though she'd been strangely hesitant to endorse the scheme—

He added: "The governor doesn't want your promise that this ship will perform as well as I claim, Sarpedon. Only that it won't be a total loss—that it won't sink when launched, for instance, or that it can be reconverted to something more conventional if necessary. You can judge that for yourself, can't you?"

"I suppose I can," the yardmaster murmured. "I suppose I can. I'd want to talk over certain items, like ballasting when there's this weight in the bows. And I'll want a model made to demonstrate these crazy fore-and-aft sails. But . . . yes, we can surely talk further."

"Good. We're bound to reach agreement."

"Oh, wonderful!" Erissa hugged Reid's waist.

He thought: Less wonderful than I'd hoped for. It'll keep me busy, what times you don't, my beautiful; and that's essential, or I'll go to pieces brooding. It should win me more authority, more freedom, than I've got—maybe enough that I can persuade the Minos to save . . . whatever is possible. And mainly, it's one screaming anachronism for me to be aboard, so that maybe I'll be noticed and rescued by the time travelers who'll maybe come here to watch doomsday.

For us to be aboard, Erissa?

Christmas approached.

Reid could hardly think of the solstice festival under its right name. Now Britomartis the Maiden gave birth to Asterion, who would die and be resurrected in spring, reign with his consort Rhea over summer and harvest, and fade away at last before Grandmother Dictynna. Atlantis had less need of midwinter rejoicing than they did in the gloomy northlands Reid remembered. But its people lived close to their gods. They honored the day by processions, music, dancing—in the streets, after the maidens had danced with a bull in the town arena—exchange of gifts and good wishes, finally feasts that often turned into orgies. For a month beforehand, they bustled and glowed with readymaking.

Erissa took Reid around as much as her duties and his shipyard work allowed. The purpose was to sound out prospective crewmen; but in this season especially, he and she were apt to be welcomed with wine, an invitation to dinner, and conversation afterward until all hours. The motive wasn't only that her presence was considered to bring luck to a house and he was a celebrity—would have become more of one were he less withdrawn, less inclined to sad reveries. The Atlanteans were glad of any new face, any fresh word; their whole spirit was turned outward.

Often he couldn't help sharing their gaiety and Erissa's. Something might yet be done to rescue them, he would think. The construction project was going well, and fascinating in its own right. So if several rhytons had eased him, and Erissa sat gazing at him with lamplight soft upon her, and an old skipper had just finished some tremendous yarn about a voyage to

Colchis, the Tin Islands, the Amber Sea . . . once, by God, storm-driven to what had to be America, and a three-year job of building a new vessel after the Painted Men were persuaded to help, and a long haul home across the River Ocean . . . he would loosen up and tell them, from his country, what he guessed they could most easily understand.

Afterward, walking to their boat, the links they bore guttering in the night and now lifting her out of shadow, now casting her back: he wasn't sure if he himself understood any longer what he had been talking about.

The day after solstice dawned clear and quiet. In the town and the farmsteads they slept off their celebrations, on the isle their devotions. Reid, who had had little of either, woke early. Wandering down dew-soaked garden paths, he found Erissa waiting for him. "I hoped you would come." He could scarcely hear her. The lashes moved along her cheekbones. "This is . . . a free time . . . for everyone. I thought—I packed food—I thought we might—"

They rowed, not to the city but to a spot beyond which she indicated. Their route passed through the shadow of the volcano; but it too was still this day, and little silvery fish streaked the water. Having tied the boat, they hiked across a ridge, the narrowest on Atlantis, to the seacoast. She knew these hills as well as did any of the bulls they glimpsed, majestically dreaming near hay-filled racks in an otherwise empty huge landscape. A trail led them to a cove on the southern shore. Cliffs enclosed it, save where they opened on a blueness that sparkled to the horizon. Closer at hand the water was green and gold, so clear that you could see pebbles on the bottom yards from the sandy beach. Wavelets lapped very gently; here was no wind. The dark bluffs drank sunlight and gave it back.

Erissa spread a cloth and on it bread, cheese, apples, a flagon of wine and two cups. She wore a plain skirt and in this sheltered place had thrown off shoes and cloak alike. "How peaceful the world is," she said.

Reid gusted a sigh.

She considered him. "What do you mourn, Duncan? That you may never win home again? But—" He saw the reddening; she grew quite busy laying out their picnic. "But you can find a new home. Can't you?"

"No," he said.

She gave him a stricken look. "Why, is there someone?" And he realized he had never mentioned Pamela to her.

"I haven't told you," he blurted. "The Ariadne desired me not to. But I think—I know—I'm not here for nothing."

"Of course not," she breathed. "When you were brought that strangely from a land that magic."

He dared speak no further. He looked at her and she at him.

He thought: Oh, yes, explanations are cheap, and Pamela (unfair; I) would be glib with them. This girl is over-ready for a man, and here I come as a mysterious, therefore glamorous foreigner. And I, I've known her older self, and fell a ways in love, as far as I've sometimes fallen in the (my) past, which was not too far to climb back out and re-find reasonable contentment with Pamela; but how can any woman stand against the girl she once was, or any man?

He thought: Suddenly I have a new goal. To spare her what that other Erissa endured.

He thought: Those eyes, those half parted lips. She wants me to kiss her, she expects I will. And she's right. No more than that . . . today. I don't dare more, nor dare say her the whole truth. Not yet. But the older Erissa told me that we will—but that's in the future I must steer her from—but that's thinking, and I think too much, I waste these few days in thinking.

He leaned toward her. A gull mewed overhead. Light streamed off its wings.

# FOURTEEN

"Yes, your friends are doing fine," Diores said. "They send their regards."

Reid tried not to glower at him. They sat alone in an offside room of the temple, to which the American had drawn the Athenian after the latter's long private interview with Lydra. Diores' smile continued bland; he lounged back at ease on the stone bench. "Just what are they doing?" Reid asked.

"Well, Uldin's breaking horses and training men for his cavalry. Or aims to. It's slow, scarcely begun, among other reasons because he's got only the one saddle—hasn't found a leatherworker who can make 'em right, he says. Oleg . . . hm . . . shipbuilding, like I hear tell you are. I'll be mighty interested to see what you've started."

"I'm afraid that's forbidden," Reid answered. "State secret."

It wasn't, but he meant to contact the governor and have the declaration made immediately. Why give the enemy a break? And Theseus was the enemy, who would pull down Erissa's sunny cosmos unless somehow history could be amended.

No, not even that. Wouldn't the legends and the archeology be the same, three or four thousand years hence, if Minoan Crete lived a little longer? Not much longer; the lifetime of a girl; was that unreasonable to ask of the gods?

"Why are you here?" he demanded. "And a picked crew." They were no ordinary sailors, he'd heard, but warriors of the royal household, who kept to themselves and scarcely spoke to the Atlanteans.

"As to that last," Diores drawled, "you don't get common seamen who'll travel in winter. Too risky." As if to bear him out, wind hooted and rain plashed beyond the richly tapestried walls.

"Oleg says he can build a year-round ship, but meanwhile we use what we've got, right?"

"You haven't told me what brought you."

"Can't, either. Sorry, mate. I carry a confidential message. You'll quite likely see me here a few times more. I will say this. Your oracle ordered Athens and Knossos should pull closer together. Fine. But how? What kind of alliance and divvy-up? Why should the Minos want to raise us from vassalage? What trouble could the envy of others cause? That sort of question. It's got to be explored; and statecraft don't work when it's put right out in public view; and seeing as how Theseus has a friend in the Ariadne, wouldn't you agree she's the logical person to begin talking with? Let's say they're feeling each other out."

Diores snickered. "She's not too long in the tooth for a man to feel," he went on. "About that, I hear you're running around with a right tasty morsel yourself."

Reid bridled. "Erissa's a bull-dancer."

"Same's your lady love of the same name used to be, hm? Makes me think there's something special here somewhere. By the way, you haven't asked me about her."

Reid wondered: Was I afraid to? Aloud: "Well?"

"She's not doing badly either. Moped a lot at first, but lately—Remember Peneleos?" Diores nudged Reid and winked. "He's been giving her what she needs. You don't mind, do you?"

"No," Reid said faintly.

Old Erissa had been through many hands. It was the maiden whom he hoped to save.

"No," Lydra said, "I will not tell you what passes between Theseus and me. You're presumptuous to ask."

"But he's part of the danger!" Reid protested.

She looked down at him from her elevated throne. Behind her lean body and stern countenance, the Griffin Judge awaited the dead. "How do you know?"

"B-b-by my foreknowledge."

"What then of the oracle commanding alliance?" Her tone

cracked like a blow across his ears. "Or did you lie about that?"

Lamps flickered in a cold space that besides they two held only shadows. But guards waited beyond the door. They were unarmed; no weapons might be brought to the sacred isle. However, four strong men could quickly make a prisoner of Duncan Reid.

"Criminals go to the quarries on Crete," Lydra said. "They do not live long. Nor do they wish to."

"I did not—My lady, I—I asked for this audience before Diores leaves b-b-because I suspect him and his master—"

"On what grounds? Aegeus rebelled but is now a dotard. Theseus slew his Cretan-raised cousins but then turned into a dutiful prince. He will become the same kind of king."

"I listened—to what they, the Achaeans, what they were saying—"

"Oh, yes. They grumble, they bluster, no doubt a few of them plot, but to what end? Theseus can be expected to keep a rein on them, the more so if he may hope to win a higher place in the Thalassocracy for himself and his realm." Lydra stabbed a finger at Reid. "Are you trying to sow discord, outlander? Whom do you serve?"

He thought: I have to tell her the truth, whatever the risk. There's no choice left.

"My lady," he said slowly, "I never lied to you, but I did hold back certain matters. Please remember, I'm a complete stranger here. I had to find out what the situation is, the rights and wrongs, the ins and outs. Including whether you would believe the whole story. I don't yet know that. But will you listen?"

She nodded.

"The reason I can prophesy," he said, "is that I come from the future."

"The what?" She frowned, trying to understand. The Keftiu language didn't lend itself well to such a concept.

But she caught the idea faster than he had hoped. And apart from signing herself and kissing her talisman, she was curiously little shaken. He wondered if she, living in a world of myth and mystery, looked on this as only another miracle.

"Yes," she murmured, "that explains a great deal."

And later: "Knossos will indeed fall? The Thalassocracy will be less than a legend?" She turned about and stared long at the portrait of the Judge. "Well," she said low, "all things are mortal."

Reid went on, describing what he could of the basic problem. His chief omission was the fact that the two Erissas were identical. He feared the possible consequences to the girl. It seemed merely needful to be vague about the date from which the woman came. The name was not uncommon and Lydra was being given a monstrous lot else to think about. He also skipped the tradition that she, traitress to the Minos, would herself be betrayed. It looked too insulting, thus too dangerous.

"What you tell me," she said, flat-voiced, "is that the gods decree Theseus shall overthrow the sea empire."

"No, my lady. The single thing I'm certain of is that the volcano will wipe out Atlantis within months, the Cretans will be conquered, and a story will tell how *a* Theseus killed a monster in Knossos. The facts need not hang together very closely. The tale could be quite false. I know already it's wrong in several ways at least. No one Minotaur ever existed, half human and half brute, just a series of sacrificial bulls. The youths and maidens from Athens are not slain but well treated. Ariadne is not the king's daughter. The Labyrinth is not a maze imprisoning the Minotaur, simply the chief palace of your priest-king, the House of the Double Ax. I could go on, but you must understand my meaning. Why should the Thalassocracy not survive the foundering of this island, perhaps for many generations?"

"If its holy of holies is destroyed by divine will, then the wrath of the gods is upon the people of the Minos," Lydra said quietly.

"They could lose heart on that account," Reid agreed. "But I swear, my lady, the causes will be as natural as . . . as a rock happening to fall on a man's head."

"Is that man not fated to die by that rock?"

Reid warned himself: You're dealing with an alien world-view. Don't stop to argue.

He said, "We can't be sure what's ordained for Crete. Asterion wills men to strive bravely to the end. Evacuating your folk to safety can be our way of striving."

Lydra sat still; she might have been carved from the same marble as her throne, and in the dull uneasy light she had scarcely more color.

"The mainlanders *could* use the chance to seize your cities," Reid plodded on. "If they do, they might regret it when the destruction comes. But we ought to plan against that event too. Everything, both the old story I read and what I have seen and heard in this age, everything makes me doubt Theseus." He paused. "And that's why I asked what message he has sent you, my lady."

Lydra remained moveless, expressionless. Reid had started wondering if something was wrong with her when she said: "I'm sworn to secrecy. The Ariadne cannot violate her oath. However, you may have guessed that he is . . . interested in the idea of closer relationships with the Labyrinth . . . and would naturally see if I might be persuaded to help."

"Diores told me that much, my lady. Uh, uh, could you keep him in play? Prolong negotiations, immobilize him till the crisis is past?"

"You have been heard, Duncan. But the Ariadne must decide. I will not receive you soon again."

And suddenly, strangely, Lydra's shoulders bowed. She passed a hand across her eyes and whispered, "It is no easy thing being the Ariadne. I thought . . . I believed, when the vision came to me in that hallowed place . . . I believed priestesshood would be unending happiness and surely the high priestess lived in the eternal radiance of Asterion. Instead—endless rites, endlessly the same—drab squabbles and intrigues—whisker-chinned crones who abide and abide, while the maidens come and serve and go home to be brides—" She straightened. "Enough. You are dismissed. Speak no word of what has passed between us."

They sought their cove on another day. "Let's swim," Erissa said, and was unclad and in the water before he could answer. Her hair floated black on its clarity, her limbs white below. "Nyah, afraid of cold?" she shouted, and splashed at him.

What the hell, he decided, and joined her. The water was in truth chilly. He churned it to keep warm. Erissa dove, grabbed his ankle and pulled him under. It ended in a laughing, gasping wrestling match.

When they went ashore the breeze made them shiver again. "I know a cure for this," Erissa said, and came into his embrace. They lay down on a blanket. Presently she grinned. "You've stronger medicine in mind, haven't you?"

"I, I can't help it. O gods, but you're beautiful!"

She said, gravely and trustingly, "You can have me whenever you want, Duncan."

He thought: I'm forty and she's seventeen. I'm American and she's Minoan. I'm of the Atomic Age and she's of the Bronze Age. I'm married, I have children, and she's a virgin. I'm an old idiot and she's the springtime that never was in my life before she came.

"That wouldn't be good for you, would it?" he managed to ask.

"What better?" She pressed against him.

"No, hold off, seriously, you'd be in trouble, wouldn't you?"

"Well—I am half consecrated while I'm here as a dancer— But I don't care, I don't care!"

"I do. I must. We'd better put our clothes on."

He thought: We have to survive. Until what? Until we know if her country will. Afterward—If it does, will I stay here? If it doesn't, will I bring her home with me? Can I do either? May I?

His tunic and her skirt resumed, they sat back down. She snuggled. Her fingers ruffled his beard. "You're always sorrowful, down underneath, aren't you?" she asked.

"I have some knowledge of what is to be," he replied, though he dared not get specific, "and it does hurt."

"Poor darling god! I do think you're a god, even if you won't admit it. Must you live every unhappiness twice? Why not every happiness, then? Look, the sky's blue and the water's green and the sand's soaked full of sunshine and here's a beaker of wine . . . no, let me hold it to your lips, I want your arm around my waist and your other hand right here—"

A good many compromises had had to be made as work progressed on the ship, some with Keftiu prejudices and requirements, some with the limitations of local technology, some with aspects of hydrodynamics that Reid discovered he had not known about. The end result was smaller, less handy, and less conspicuously extratemporal than he had hoped.

However, it was a considerable achievement. About eighty feet long, the slender hull was built outward and upward from a great dugout. Down the center ran a raised and bulwarked deck, beneath which passed thwarts for the rowers. The ram was a beak projecting at the waterline, bronze-sheathed, backed by heavy timbers. The twenty oars on either side were interrupted at the middle by leeboards which had turned out to be more practical, on the whole, than a false keel or centerboard. Steering was by a true rudder. Two masts bore fore-and-aft rigs. Because Sarpedon insisted—probably rightly, in view of the low freeboard, the scanty ballasting, and the impacts sustained in battle—that they be readily unstepped, the masts were short. Reid gained sail area by using gaffs, and he had available both a genoa jib and a spinnaker; but the Minoan cloth, loosely woven, inclined to stretch and sag and absorb water, did not give the performance of canvas or dacron.

Thus the handling characteristics turned out so odd to him that his crew caught the knack about as fast as he did. Before long they were taking practice cruises on virtually every day of halfway decent weather. They were a hearty, laughter-loving two score and ten, youngsters in the late teens and early twenties, delighted at this novelty, bound and determined to master their ship and lay their wake in rings around those old fogies who grumbled at new-fangled foreign foolishness. No longer needed as an instructor, Reid usually stayed behind with Erissa. Time for him and her was shrinking unbearably. And one of his sailors, a slim youth of good looks and good family, who could scarcely keep his eyes off the girl, was named Dagonas.

But she came aboard with Reid for the final test, the test of the ram, before the vessel was officially dedicated. The governor had released a hulk, traded to the state for cannibalizing by a merchant owner who hadn't considered it worth his while to make those repairs which Sarpedon now carried out. A rival gang, envious boys and skeptical shellbacks, agreed to man the target craft and show up the radicals. Boats came along to rescue whoever got dunked.

It was clear and brisk offshore, whitecaps marching, the by now almost permanent black column out of Pillar Mountain shredded by a gleefully piping wind. Overhead trailed a flight of storks, homeward bound from Egypt to the northlands, heralds of spring. The ram ship leaped and rolled. Its sides were gay with red and blue stripes; on the sails were embroidered dolphins. The waters rushed, the timbers talked, the rigging harped.

Erissa, forward on the upper deck beside Reid, clapped her hands. The hair streamed back off her shoulders, the skirt was pressed against her loins. "Oh, see!" she cried happily. The vessel came about in a rattle of booms, gaffs, and blocks. It had just passed the bows of the conventional ship, which trudged along on oars, unable to come anywhere near the wind.

"Stop your fancyfooting and let's have some action!" bawled the distant skipper.

"Well, I suppose we should," Reid told Sarpedon, "having proved they can't lay a grapnel on us." They looked at each other in shared unsureness. The boys on the thwarts raised a yell.

Standing off, the rammers lowered sail, racked masts, and broke out oars. The target crew poised uneasily at their own oars. They knew what happened in a collision. Both hulls were stove in, along with the ribs of any rowers who didn't get clear.

Reid went aft to his quartermaster. "You remember the drill," he said. "Aim for the center, but not straight. That could leave us hung up on them. The idea is to rip out the strakes and sheer off."

"Like a bull goring a bear," Erissa said.

"May that be no evil omen for you, Sister," the man responded.

"Gods forfend!" Dagonas called at his bench just below. Erissa smiled down upon him. Reid saw how smooth and lithe the boy's body was. His own—well, he kept in fair shape. And Erissa was clutching his hand.

The craft began to move. The coxswain's chant gathered speed until water seethed white and the hull sprang forward. Abruptly the target was horrible in its nearness. As directed, it tried to take evasive action. As expected, the rudder-and-tiller combination was so much more efficient than steering oars that no escape was possible.

Reid's people had rehearsed the maneuver often, against nets supported on logs. Oars on the inner side snapped erect; those on the outer continued driving. The noise and shock were less than he had anticipated. Disengaging was awkward—obviously more practice needed there—but it was managed. By then, the struck galley lay heeled far over. Wooden and unloaded, it didn't sink; but presently it floated awash and the waves were pounding it to pieces.

Cheers pealed from the victors. The vanquished were too busy swimming to the boats for a response. Reid and Sarpedon made a thorough inspection. "No harm that I can see," the yardmaster declared. "This ship by itself could drive off a fleet." He embraced the American. "What you've done! What you've done!"

Erissa was there. "You *are* a god," she sobbed. They dared not kiss in public, but she knelt and held him around the knees.

Again Atlantis swarmed with preparations for festival. But this was the great one. In the resurrection of Asterion lay that of the world and its dead.

First he must die and be mourned. Forty days before the vernal equinox, the Keftiu hooded altars, screened off caves and springs, bore through the streets their three holy symbols reversed and draped in black, rent their garments, gashed their flesh, and cried on Dictynna for mercy. For thirty days thereafter, most of them abstained from meat, wine, and sexual intercourse; and in their homes, lamps burned perpetually so that beloved ghosts might find the way back.

Not that business stopped. After all, seaborne traffic was starting up again. And however devout, the Keftiu were incapable of long faces for many hours in a row. And the last ten of the forty days were to be pure celebration. The god would not yet have come from hell to claim that Bride Who was also his Mother and Grandmother, but man's forward-looking joy helped make sure that he would.

Beneath somberness and decorum, excitement bubbled even on the temple isle. Soon the maidens would take ship for Knossos, to dance with the bulls and the youths: soon, soon. Erissa worked her class daily. Reid stood by, gnawing his nails.

Why did Lydra keep refusing to see him? She couldn't be that busy. Lord knew she had ample time for Diores, when the Achaean showed up on his frequent missions. Why was she doing nothing about evacuation? She said, when Reid got together the boldness to grab a chance to drop her a few words that she and he alone understood, she said she was in touch with the Minos; and true, boats shuttled across the sixty-mile channel between, written messages borne by male old-timers in her service who were both illiterate and close-mouthed; she said the matter was under advisement, she said, she said.

Meanwhile the volcano spewed smoke and, ever oftener, flames. Its fine ash made the fields dusty. Sometimes at night you saw fresh lava flow glowing from the mouth; next morning you saw new grotesqueries on those black flanks, and steam puffing white from fumaroles. The ground shivered, the air rumbled. In the taverns men spoke dogmatically and at length of what precautions should be taken against the possibility of a major eruption. Reid didn't notice that anybody actually did much. Of course, they never imagined what the blowup was going to be like. He himself couldn't.

If he could tell them!

Well, at worst there were plenty of well-found boats. Practically every Atlantean family owned one and could put to sea, provisioned, on a few hours' notice. But they couldn't keep the sea too long; and he didn't know just when the hammer would fall; and he did know that the time was very short now for him and Erissa to stand on a starlit hilltop, so close together that Pamela and children couldn't get in between, and for her to breathe, "We'll be wedded right after the festival, right after, my darling, my god," while the mountain growled at his back unheeded save for the glow it cast upon her.

Rain fell anew, but gently, little more than a springtime mist that quickened the earth and if it lasted until morning would not hinder the procession of the maidens to the ships for Crete. But beyond its coolness and the damp odors it awoke lay absolute night.

Lydra confronted Reid beneath the Griffin Judge. In the lamplight her black gown was like another shadow, against which her face thrust startlingly white. From her throne she said: "I summoned you this late on purpose, exile. There are none to hear us but the guards beyond the door."

Reid knew with a chill: There need never be any to eavesdrop. The door is thick. Though not too thick for those men to hear a call. And they are wholly vowed to her service.

"What has my lady in mind?" he got forth.

"This," the Ariadne told him. "You thought to embark tomorrow with your giddy Erissa, did you not? It shall not be. You will remain here."

Suddenly he knew that his cage had no doors.

"You have been less than candid," she said. "Did you imagine Diores and I would never talk about your companions in Egypt and so learn what you were withholding about the woman? These are uncanny matters. If you did not tell the whole truth, how can we suppose you did not lie? That you are not the enemy of him the gods have chosen, Prince Theseus?"

"My lady," he heard himself cry, "Theseus is making a tool of you. He'll abandon you as soon as you're not needed—"

"Hold your mouth or you're dead!" she yelled. "Guards! Guards, to me!"

He knew, he knew: Long before, the man with the lion eyes had come into her aloneness and promised her what no other man would have dared, that he would make her his queen if he could; but for this, she must needs aid him in bringing about the downfall of her king.

Why didn't I see it? He shrieked in his head. Because I wasn't used to intrigue, but mainly because I didn't want to kick apart the glittery little paradise she let me spin around myself, he whispered in his head.

He realized: When she passed on to Diores and so to Theseus the word I gave her, that was Lydra's required service—that, and whatever help she's been lending to a conspiracy among the metics and the disaffected on Crete, and now her locking me away lest I break the silence.

Through how many springtime nights, while her maidens dreamed and whispered in their dormitory of the young men they would meet, through how many years has she prayed for a chance like this? And to what gods?

# FIFTEEN

THE SHIPS were coming in. Already the Piraeus strand was full and newcomers must lie out at anchor. There too was Oleg's great vessel; it could be beached, but with difficulty, and the Russian wanted to avoid curiosity seekers, thieves, and blabber-mouths as much as possible. Most crews pitched tents on the nearby shore and walked to Athens for sightseeing and amuse-ment. But on any given day, many men lounged in those camps.

Ribald shouts blew around Erissa with the smoke of cookfires. Several Achaeans approached her as she came striding. She ignored them, though she felt their stares on her back. A woman —bonny, too—who swung along that arrogantly—unescorted? What could she be, if not one of the whores come down to ply their trade? But she spurned every offer. So maybe she had a rendezvous with some important man in his tent? But the chief-tains weren't squatted here, they were in town at the inns, the mightiest at the palace. . . . The warriors shrugged and re-turned to their roasting spits, their dice games, their contests of speed and strength and bragging.

She came to a row of skiffs. Each had a ferryman on standby, whose boredom vanished when she appeared. "Who'll take me out to yonder ship?" she asked, pointing at Oleg's.

Eyes went up and down her height. Teeth shone wet in beards. "What for?" someone asked knowingly. "What pay?" laughed his companion. "Mine's the boat belongs to it," said a third, "and I'll take you, but you'll earn your passage. Agreed?"

Erissa remembered the barbarians of Thrace, the burghers of Rhodes, and too many more. She drew herself erect, widened her eyes till the pupils were circled in white, and willed pallor into her face. "I have business concerning the Beings," she said in her coldest witch-voice. "Behave yourselves—" she stabbed a ges-ture—"unless you want that manhood you boast of more than you use to blacken and drop off."

They backed away, terrified, scrabbling out shaky little signs of their own. She gestured at Oleg's man. He all but crawled to help her aboard, pushed his craft afloat, and worked at the oars like a thresher, never lifting his glance to her.

She muted a sigh. How easy to dominate, when you had ceased being frightened for yourself.

Oleg's rubicund visage and golden beard burned in sunlight

reflected off water, as he peered over the bulwark. "Who the *chawrt*— Why, you, Erissa! Saints alive, I haven't seen you for weeks! Come aboard, come aboard. Hoy, you scuts!" he bellowed. "Drop a rope ladder for my lady."

He took her into a cabin, set her down on a bunk, poured wine that a crewman had fetched, and clanged his beaker against hers. "Good to greet you, lass." The cabin being a mere hutch cluttered with his personal gear, he joined her on the bunk. Windows were lacking, but enough light seeped past the door for her to make him out. It was warm; she felt the radiation of his shaggy tunic-clad body and drank the odor of his sweat. Waves clinked against the hull, which rocked slightly. Outside, feet thudded, voices shouted, tackle creaked, as the work of preparation continued which he had been overseeing.

"You needn't look that grim, need you?" he rumbled.

"Oleg." She caught his free hand. "This host Theseus is summoning. Where are they bound?"

"You know that. Been announced. A plundering trip to Tyrrhenian waters."

"Are they really, though? This sudden—this many allies—"

He squinted pityingly at her. "I understand. You fear for Crete. Well, look. You'd not get the Atticans, not to speak of what other Achaeans they've talked into joining—you won't get them to attack any place under the protection of the Minos. They aren't crazy. At the same time, they do grow restless, and the Minos finds advantage in letting them work that off now and then, on folk who've naught to offer in the market but slaves and who themselves are apt to play pirate. Right?"

"But this year of all years," she whispered.

Oleg nodded. "I went along with the notion, when my advice was asked. If we really are in for a tidal wave as Duncan claims, I'd hate to see fine ships wrecked, most especially my lovely new dromon. Let's get them out of harm's way. How I look forward to showing Duncan my work! His idea, you recall, that we build something really up-to-date that'd catch the notice of the time wizards."

"Who has warned the Minos about the disaster to come?" Erissa demanded.

"Well, you heard Diores yourself, relating what he'd seen and done on Atlantis. Duncan's an honored guest there. I got a couple of Diores' men drunk and asked them out, just to make sure. It's true. So surely by now he must've put the word across.

"We'd not have heard, here in Athens. If the Cretans do mean to empty their cities and scatter their navy well out at sea, they'd hardly give advance notice, would they? That'd be asking for trouble. I'd not be surprised but what Gathon, under orders, put the flea in Theseus' ear about organizing a joint Achaean expedition beyond Italy. Beyond temptation, ha, ha!"

"Then why do I remember that my country was destroyed this spring?" she asked.

Oleg stroked her hair as her father might have done. "Maybe you misremember. You've said things are blurry where they aren't blank for you, right around the day of the downfall."

"There is nothing unclear about my memories of the aftermath."

"Well, so maybe the God's changed his mind and sent us back to save Crete." Oleg crossed himself. "I'm not so bold as to claim that, mark you. I'm just a miserable sinner trying to make an honest profit. But a priest of the God told me men are free to choose, that there is no foreordained doom except the very Last Day. Meanwhile we can only walk the way we hope is best, a step at a time."

The palm crossing her head reminded her of the new white streaks which had come into her locks this winter. On Atlantis, those tresses shone like a midnight sky.

"Anyway," Oleg said, "remember, we've kept our mouths shut to the Athenians. *They don't know the future.* If they believe anything, it's that they're bound to get friendlier with Knossos.

"For proof, consider that Theseus won't be leading this expedition though he instigated it. His idea must be to bleed off as much Achaean restlessness as possible while he's away. If he looked for ruin to strike Crete, would he hie himself there?"

"That was the news which frightened me till I had to seek you, Oleg." Erissa stared at the bulkhead. "When the prince made known that he would be among the next hostages—"

The Russian nodded. "Yes, I've heard Duncan's notion. I worried too for a while. But then I thought, first, Theseus and what malcontents and crooks he might gather, what could they do in the Minos' own city except get themselves killed? Second, like I said, he's got no reason to think the Labyrinth will face trouble from the elements. Third, if he hopes to dicker for a better standing in the Thalassocracy, what shrewder way than to settle down some years in an honored post, where they'll try to win his good will against the day he goes home? Fourth, I wouldn't be surprised if Gathon, again, dropped hints it'd pay him to come. You see, if Duncan's warned the Minos about Theseus, it's purely natural for the Minos to want Theseus in the Labyrinth where they can keep an eye on him. And fifth, lass, this dromon's going to be the flagship of the Tyrrhenian outing. Admiral Diores will travel on it, and *I'll* keep an eye on *him*."

He hugged her lightly. "Yes, we're in a dangerous world," he said. "It never was anything else, and never will be. But I do believe you've reason to feel some cheer."

He would have been glad to entertain her a while, but when she failed to convince him he was wrong, she excused herself as fast as possible. Walking back to Athens, she found a cypress grove along the road where she could hide and weep.

She hoped no one could tell that when she continued.

Driving a chariot of Diores his chieftain, Peneleos was among the warriors who had gone forth to summon men off their scattered farmsteads. He returned on the day after Erissa's visit to Oleg: shouting for joy as he clattered up the Acropolis, horses tramping, bronze gleaming, cloak blowing behind him with speed, his own half-naked attendants toiling afoot in his dust. Erissa was in the crowd of underlings who stopped work to watch the splendid spectacle. Light off his helmet and breastplate speared her eyes.

Now? she thought. This very night?

Quite likely. Uldin is back too, sulkier than I dared await.

She felt acutely aware of everything around her, shadows between cobblestones, flies over an odorous dungheap by the
stables, silver-gray of shakes on the palace roof and of sunlit
smoke rising from them, a yelping dog, gowns and tunics surrounding her—though the wearers were only other objects, their
words only other noises. Her thoughts moved coolly above, ob-
serving, weighing, fitting together. Beneath lay that sense of fate
which had risen in her during the winter.

Briefly, yesterday, she had hoped, just a tiny bit. . . . Well,
she would not surrender. She *knew* Theseus' voyage to Knossos
was in the pattern. She did not know how, or know what the
Ariadne might have to do with it. She had been unable to persuade Oleg that those two were in conspiracy. Doubtless her
failure was itself part of the pattern, whose weaving went on.
But she *knew* that, one way or another, she would rejoin Duncan before the end. For over the months, staring into mirrors,
groping in a haze of half-recollections, she had come to recognize
a face among those which were around her at that final moment;
and it was her own.

Was she herself, then, the witch who had taken the last hours
out of those memories which were to nourish her over the years?

Why would she do so? Would she? It did not make sense. And
thus it might be the one loose thread that, by her refusal to do
the thing, she could seize to unravel the whole web. If she, cast
back into this age after another quarter century, knew what she
in this house could tell her younger self—

During her life with Dagonas, she had inquired of travelers as
earnestly as of any of the remaining Keftiu: What happened?
They told her different versions, which mostly had the same
skeleton. Theseus and the other hostages were newly in Knossos
when earthquake smote and the sea destroyed the Minoan fleet.
He gathered people (whom he claimed an oracle had told him to
organize) and seized the shattered capital by force. His own
ships and those of his allies, spared because they had been far

out to sea, arrived shortly after to reinforce him. Having imposed his will on what was left of the main Cretan cities, he went home, taking the Ariadne along. Many stories said she did not appear to have left unwillingly.

In the past—her past, which lay futureward of today—Erissa had considered that unlikely. It didn't fit what she had known of Lydra. Besides, Theseus showed at Naxos that the priestess was nothing to him. Poor creature, she ended her days in a mystery cult, one of those ancient dark faiths whose devotees gave themselves by turn to orgy and torture. Theseus went on to unite a large mainland domain under his rule. The news that he came at last to an unhappy end of his own was colorless consolation.

Erissa nodded. The pattern was clearing before her. It had been clearing throughout the winter, as Diores traveled back and forth between Athens and Atlantis. The Ariadne must in truth be aiding Theseus, just as in those dim traditions Duncan had related. No doubt the disclosures out of time had inspired her.

But Erissa could not say this aloud—accusations would only earn her a slit throat—and Oleg and Uldin were nearly always off on their business, and when they were at the palace she was never alone with either of them, and she could scarcely hope to repeat her trick of the Periboean grove, suspicious as the court was of her.

Yesterday, when most men of the royal household were gone, she had seized the opportunity to seek out Oleg. But she had failed to make the Russian comprehend how a mere story told by one who claimed to be an exile from the future (and did, to be sure, have some remarkable things to show) could affect people who believed in fate. Oleg did not; his curious god forbade him. Theseus and Lydra—who *wanted* faith in their high and liberating destiny—would stake everything they had, the life of the whole Athenian kingly house and state, on what Oleg could only see as an insane gamble that everything would work out exactly right. Since he knew Theseus, Diores, and the rest were hardheaded men like himself, he cast aside Erissa's fears.

Moreover, while he appreciated what he had seen of Cretan refinement and might well prefer to live there; and while he was fond of her; what really was her country to him? If he could not go home, he could make a new life in Greece. He had already started.

That busyness had helped keep him from thinking about the pattern. Erissa, immured in the round of an Achaean woman, had had ample chances to brood, puzzle out a few of the paradoxes, and slowly weave her own web whose threads she must soon draw together.

Yes, most likely this very night.

Peneleos came to their room earlier after sunset than she had expected. She rose, smiling, shaking back her hair across the Egyptian shift he had given her. "I thought you would drink late in the hall after being afield," she greeted.

He laughed. The lamplight showed him big, thickly muscled, face a trifle wine-flushed but eyes bright and posture steady. Beneath the yellow locks, that face was boyishly round and soft of beard. "Tomorrow night I may," he said. "But I've missed you more than any feasting."

They embraced. His mouth and hands were less clumsy than they had been the first few times, and she used every skill that hers possessed. Inwardly she was cold with destiny. What flutterings went through her were because she was on her way to Duncan.

"Now, nymph, now," he said low in his throat.

Usually she had let herself enjoy their encounters. Why not? They were a small reason, among larger ones, for luring him in the first place—to be free of that hunger, at least, while she waited half prisoner in Athens. In the beginning he was awed and bewildered. (Diores had encouraged him when the older man noticed what was developing. The admiral would like few things better than having a trusty follower live with, watch, and, if need be, curb this woman whose part and power in the world were unknown but were beyond doubt witchy and none too friendly.) Later Peneleos gained confidence; but he stayed kind to her in his self-centered Achaean fashion. She liked him well enough.

Tonight she must give him all her art and none of her feeling. She must bring him to a calm and happy drowsiness but not let it glide into natural slumber.

The lamp was guttering when she raised herself on an elbow. "Rest, my lover," she crooned, over and over, and her fingers moved on his body in slow rhythm and when the gaze she had trapped began to turn glassy she began blinking her own eyes in exact tune with his heartbeat.

He went quickly under. Already in the grove he had not been hard to lay the Sleep on. That fact had caused her to choose him among the unwed men she regularly saw, and seduce him, after her plan had taken vague shape. Each time thereafter that she ensorcelled him—in guise of lulling him or easing a headache or bringing on a pleasant dream—made the next time easier. She was sure he followed the command she always gave: Do not tell anyone about this that we are doing together; it is a dear and holy secret between us; rather, forget that I did more than murmur to you, until I do it again.

Now she sat staring down at him in the wan, flickering light. His features were too firmly made to fall slack, but something had gone out of them and out of the half-closed eyes. It had not gone far, though. It lay back in the darkness of the skull, like one of those snakes fed by Keftiu householders who believed their dead came home in that form. After hours it would rouse and uncoil; and the wrong sounds could bring it instantly awake and striking.

In the Sleep you believed and did what you were told, up to a point—and she thought her repeated suggestions that he acted out had driven that point further up than it stood in most men—but you would not do anything that your undeceived waking self would recognize as wrong or dangerous. She must be totally careful tonight.

The lamp was almost out. She rose, cat-cautious, and replenished it. The room was warm, thick with odors of oil, smoke, flesh, and musky breath. Outside the door curtain were darkness and silence.

Erissa leaned over him. "Peneleos," she said, word by soft and measured word, "you know I am your woman who wants only to serve you. But you know I also serve the Goddess."

"Yes," he responded, toneless as always before.

"Hear me, Peneleos. The Goddess has revealed to me that the divine plan, Hers and Zeus', for the union of our two peoples is imperiled. If that be done which is forbidden, the everlasting curse will fall upon them. Tell me what is intended so I may warn against wrongness."

She held her breath till he responded. Her hope pivoted on the likelihood that Diores had confided in him. Surely more men than the prince and admiral would have to know the real scheme if it differed from the announced one. Peneleos, while young, was not indiscreet; and information would enable him to keep sharper watch on whatever his leman might be doing or learning.

The answers she drew forth clenched her sense of fate. Winter-long plotting between Theseus, Lydra, and those whom Lydra's agents had discovered or planted in Knossos; story of the future drawn from a too trusting Duncan Reid; reinterpretation of the Periboean oracle to mean that the Goddess Herself desired the triumph of Athens; scheme to seize the queen city and command the whole fleet to turn about and fall on Keft; safety margin, that no hostile move need be made if disaster did not grab the Labyrinth when it was supposed to; everything kept secret from the Minos; Duncan left behind under guard on some pretext—

She didn't pause for bitterness. Much of this she had suspected for weeks.

"Hark," she said. "You remember that you have fretted about possible trouble from the man Uldin. Know now that Poseidon is angered at misuse of the horse—that his sacred animal should be ridden like a donkey!—and will bring ruin on the expedition unless the sacrilege ceases for good. Uldin must be slain in expiation: but secretly, for if the reason were given out, messengers would leave for Crete."

She took her time, repeating, elaborating, until she felt she had engraved belief on the ill-defended mind. Moonset and sunrise drew nearer with each breath, but she *knew* she would see Duncan again. In the end, she left Peneleos on the bed, in the dark, while she went "to fetch your lord Diores so we can plan what to do."

The rush-strewn passage was cold under her bare feet. Shadows jumped around the streaming lampflame. Uldin's room was a few doors down. She entered. He lay snoring beside a new slave girl, his first being too heavy with child. (I will not have another by Duncan, went through Erissa's thoughts like a bat that flies forth every twilight. I seem to have become barren since the last one Dagonas gave me. Welladay, I could not have done what I have done here were matters otherwise; let the memory of Deukalion comfort me. Unless, after this strife is over, Rhea will grant—) The Hun had kept to his shaven head, three tufts of hair, and barbaric earrings. The scarred coarse visage was hideous to her. But where else was help?

She shook him. He came immediately awake. She laid a hand across his mouth, stooped, and whispered: "Rise at once. I've laid the Sleep on Peneleos and learned something terrible."

He nodded and followed her, unclad but gripping his iron blade.

Early in winter, still dwelling alone and remembering Duncan much too well, she had recalled a thing he told her. In future centuries Dorian tribesmen from the north were to overrun the Achaeans because their iron weapons were cheap enough that any man could bear them, whereas a full bronze panoply was only for a nobleman. So later she asked Peneleos: "Are your leaders wise to let Uldin create the horse archers he speaks of? Once that usage spreads, will it not spell the end of the war chariot, even of the whole state founded on charioteer lords?"

At intervals she strengthened the suggestion while he lay in the Sleep.

Her act had seemed nothing but a minor wedge she might drive. However, it took effect. Peneleos repeated the idea to Diores, Theseus, and others, who grew thoughtful. They did not outright forbid Uldin to carry on, but they found pretexts to gradually withdraw support until they should fully have reconsidered. In the end he sat about idle and smoldering.

Tonight, from a Peneleos who thought he was Diores, the Hun learned of a scheme to kill him. He did not learn that Erissa had anything to do with those words aside from extracting them. Peneleos had been ordered to forget that; and Uldin's acquaintance with shaman arts was limited.

"Ungh," he grunted. After a moment, he shot her a glance from a countenance otherwise gone motionless. "Why do you warn me?"

"I've also learned of a plot to fall on Crete when it lies racked and broken," she said. "The warning we bore was never allowed to reach the Minos. Those are my people. I want to save them. I can't get there alone."

"I'd wondered about that Tyrrhenian expedition."

"And think, Uldin!" Erissa seized his arm. "The mainland does have reason to fear your kind of soldier. That's why they've delayed and hampered you here. Crete, guarded by the sea, never would. Rather, they should welcome a cavalry to help control that mainland. The more so when you come as their deliverer."

He snapped to decision. "Very well. You may be deadly wrong, but if you're right, we're fools to linger here. And a man dies when the gods will." Somehow, for the moment it flashed, his grin took away his ugliness. "Besides, this gives me less sea voyaging to do."

"Go make yourself ready," Erissa said.

When he was gone, she bent again over Peneleos. "Sleep now, my love," she whispered. "All has been done. All is well." With moth gentleness she closed his eyes. "Sleep late. Forget what we have spoken of. The gods and prudence alike forbid that more than your lord Diores know. Sleep. Wake refreshed. Do not seek after me. I will only be away on an errand. Sleep deeply, Peneleos."

His breathing became still more regular. On an impulse she did not quite understand, she kissed him. Then she grew busy gathering clothes, blankets, jewelry and utensils and weapons to wrap in them.

Uldin returned, clad in his old foul-smelling outfit. He pointed at the bed. "Shall I stick him?" he asked.

"No!" Erissa realized she had answered too loudly. "No, that could start the hue and cry after us hours before it need happen. Follow me."

They had no trouble leaving palace or city. Since Athens was choked with king's men, no one saw reason to post guards. The moon was still up, approaching the full. (When that happens during Asterion's feast, the Keftiu believe it bodes an especially good year, Erissa thought; and her feeling of being an embodied purpose could not keep the sting from her eyes.) The road to the Piraeus stretched gray and empty, between silvery fields and silver-tipped shadowy trees. Stars were few. The air was cool and still, so that their footfalls crunched noisy and they lowered voices as they made what scanty plans they could.

"Walking!" Uldin spat once in disgust.

Sentries were awake at the beach, where boats and the cargoes of ships lay valuable. Uldin let Erissa pick the craft she thought best: a fifteen-footer with mast and sail. Their vessel should not be too big for him to do some rowing or sculling at need, yet sufficiently big to make Atlantis in reasonable safety. For the most part they would depend on the wind, and entirely on her navigation.

He had to bluster before he succeeded in commandeering the boat and a few provisions. But he was good at that; and as far as the warriors knew, he was still well up in royal favor. Erissa stood aside, unrecognized in a male tunic and cowled cloak of Peneleos'. The story of a secret and urgent mission that she had concocted was finally believed without sending a runner back to ask Diores. She was not surprised at that, nor at the favorable breeze they caught beyond the roadstead. For she remembered how these same planks bore her and Dagonas toward Troy.

Wind faded out at dawn. The boat lay becalmed in a nearly flat sea, which glittered across its dark blue to the rosy-clouded luminance in the east. Westward, Argolis rose in mountains and shadowy woodlands—Troezen, where Theseus was born. Attica was low on the after horizon. Elsewhere a few islands were strewn, white and green. Erissa shipped the now useless steering oar and doffed her cloak, for the dawn was fast warming.

"Best we eat," she said. "We'll be busy later."

"Or idle," Uldin growled by the mast. "We can't get far on strength alone. When'll it blow again?"

"Before long, I expect. Then we can await noontide calms, brisk afternoons and evenings, little or nothing throughout most nights."

"Ungh. And the fleet due to start forth tomorrow. They'll have rowers to overtake us, and whoever sees us may well think we're worth a closer look."

"I said we would go around behind the islands, taking cover at need. We can see a galley before it can spy us."

"Days at best, then, traveling." Uldin scratched under his shirt, caught a louse, and cracked it between his teeth. "Death along the way, not unlikely."

"If I am to meet Duncan again, as I told you long ago I would—"

"You never said I'd be there." Suddenly her heart wavered. He drew his dagger and wagged the point at her. "See here. You're an eldritch one. More so, I think, than the lover you're taking us to. I'm none too sure you didn't trick or bewitch me into coming along. And you'd cast me aside like a worn-out pair of breeches if you'd no further use for me."

"Uldin, no . . . I—"

"Keep quiet. I can take my chances with you, or I can turn around, give you to Theseus for killing after they've wrung what you know from you, and take my chances with him. Which is it to be?"

She rallied her courage. She *knew,* she did, she *knew.* With clamped fists and quick breath: "Me. You must."

"I must not do one befouled thing I'm not bound to do, and I'm not bound to you." Uldin's scowl eased. "Here's what I want. Blood brotherhood sworn between us. Faithfulness to death, you for me and I for you, by all our gods, demons, ancestors, hope of descendants, and blood of our veins that we mingle. Then I'll know I can trust you. I've never heard of its being done between man and woman, but you're different."

Relief weakened her. "Of course, Uldin. Gladly."

He grinned. "You're not that much different, however. Don't fear. I'll not stand between you and the man you're after, when you've found him. We can put that in the oath too, if you like. But meanwhile we'll be by ourselves for days, apt to get killed on any of them, and plenty of free times like now. Keep me happy."

She stared at him. "Oh, no," she pleaded.

He shrugged. "That's the price of my oath. You're setting a price on yours, you know."

She tried to recall the maiden who danced with bulls and fell in love with a god. But she couldn't. The road back was too long.

Well, she thought, Oleg was right about this much: Wherever a road may lead, you walk it a step at a time. "As you will, then," she said.

# SIXTEEN

THEY DIDN'T treat Reid disrespectfully. Lydra explained to the guards that he had been afflicted by visions which she recognized

as false and unlucky. He was forbidden to utter a word about
them and was to be gagged if he tried. But otherwise he was
simply confined to quarters. After her return she would lift the
curse off him.

In fact, since no other male guests remained, he had the freedom of that wing. Escorted, he was allowed to walk through the
gardens. From there he watched the ships depart for Knossos.

The Ariadne's galley went first, long and wide, the Horns on
its prow, the Pillar amidships, the Labrys on the sternpost. He
saw the maidens crowded eager on deck and tried to make out
Erissa—she'd be the quiet, disappointed one—but the distance
was too great for middle-aged eyes. Behind came two escorting
warcraft, then a line of ships and boats belonging to those lay
folk who could afford the trip. All were bright with paint and
pennons; wreaths hung at every rail; a breeze carried snatches
of song as well as coxswains' chants. The colors were the more
brilliant against the black mountain behind.

He was surprised that his rammer wasn't in the party. Then
he realized Lydra would have forbidden it, and no doubt its
crew, to go, on some pretext or other. Too many questions might
have gotten asked; or it might even have managed to stand off
the Achaean fleet.

So we're both left behind, Dagonas, he thought.

The fleet marched through the channel and out of Reid's
sight. That was the first of the ten festival days.

On the second, what priestesses had stayed behind were rowed
to town and conducted ceremonies. Reid saw that this involved
the fisher craft. After those were blessed they put to sea, turned
around, and came back to an elaborate reception. That must be
more or less simultaneous with Erissa's arrival at Knossos.

On the third day he saw a procession leave town for the high-
lands and wind back down some hours later: music, dancing,
and herded bulls. A guard, not unwilling to talk—for though
his assignment kept him from joining the fun, the Ariadne had
told him how much prestige and merit he gained by thus looking
after the unfortunate—explained that this was a small version

of the Grand Drive into Knossos. That night the volcano showed fireworks, awful and beautiful, till nearly dawn; thereafter it fell quiet.

On the fourth day the corridas began. They would continue for the rest of the celebration period. Atlantis was unique in that only girls took part, chosen by lot from the instructresses and those novices deemed ready. In most towns the show was comparatively modest. Knossos drew the champions of the Thalassocracy. There, on the last day, the youth and maiden judged to have performed best would dance with the best bull, which the Minos would then sacrifice; and Asterion, resurrected, would claim his Bride and beget himself.

I wonder if Erissa will win the garland of sacred lilies, Reid thought; and then: No. We're too near the end. I'm going to die when Atlantis does, and she . . .

On the fifth day he scarcely stirred from his bed, lay staring at the ceiling and thinking: What have I accomplished? Nothing except harm. Oleg and Uldin at least have skills useful in this age; they'll make their way. Erissa will survive and set herself free. I . . . I let every decision be made for me. In my smugness as a scion of the scientific era, I let myself be duped into telling the enemies of her people exactly what they needed to know. *I* brought on the fall of the Thalassocracy! The horrors my Erissa has to live through go straight back to me. . . . My Erissa? I wasn't good enough to make my rightful wife happy. But oh, yes, I was good enough to take advantage of a woman's need and faith, a girl's innocence. Atlantis, hurry and sink!

On the sixth day, after a white night, he saw that the game wasn't played quite to an end. He and Erissa, young Erissa, were to meet again and—And if nothing else, by the God who had yet to be created, he should keep trying to return home. His duty lay there. It came to him that duty was not the stern thing he had always supposed; it could be armor.

Escape, then. But how? He got Velas, the amiable guard, into conversation. Would it not be possible to visit town, attend a corrida, maybe hoist a few rhytons in the merriment that followed?

"No, sir, the Ariadne's orders were clear. Sorry, sir. I'd like to. Got a wife and kids there, you know, and believe me, they're sad about this. Youngest girl must be crying for Daddy. Just two and a half, sir, the cutest tyke—and smart? Why, let me tell you—"

That night Erissa came.

He was dreaming. He wanted to build a blastproof fallout shelter because World War Three was now unavoidable and Atlantis was a prime target area but Pamela said they couldn't afford it because Mark's teeth needed straightening and besides where would they find room for those bulls which bellowed and tried to gore her whose face he couldn't see and she sprang between their horns which were iron and clanged—

He sat up. Blackness filled his eyes. He thought: Burglars! and groped for the light switch. The scuffling in the corridor ended with a thud. He was in the temple of the Triune Goddess and his destiny was being played out.

"Duncan," ran the whisper. "Duncan, where are you?"

He swung his feet to the cold floor and groped his way forward, barking his ankle on a stool. "Here," he called hoarsely. These rooms had regular doors. When he opened his, he saw a lamp in the hand of Erissa.

She sped down the hallway. The flame was nearly blown out by her haste. But when she reached him, she could only stop and say, "Duncan," and slowly raise fingers to his cheek. They trembled. She wore a stained tunic and a knife. Her hair was in the dancer's ponytail; the white streak and its new neighbors leaped forth against surrounding shadows. He saw that she had grown thin. Her countenance was weatherbeaten and there were more lines than erstwhile in the brow and around the eyes.

He also began to shake. Dizziness passed through him. She laid her free arm around his neck and pulled his head down to her bosom. It was warm and, beneath the rank sweat of strife, smelled like the maiden's.

"Dress," she said urgently. "We must be gone before somebody comes."

Releasing him, she half turned and half shrieked. Through the murk Reid made out Uldin, squatting above the sprawled form of Velas. Blood matted the Atlantean's locks. He had been struck on the temple by the pommel of the Hun's saber. Uldin had a knee under Velas' neck and the edge to his throat.

"*No!*" Even then, Erissa remembered to set down the lamp. The same motion sent her wheeling full around and plunging up the hall. She kicked. Her heel caught Uldin's jaw. He went on his back. Snarling, he bounced to a crouch. "No!" Erissa said as if she were about to vomit. "We'll bind him, gag him, hide him in a room. But murder? Bad enough bringing weapons to Her isle."

Uldin came erect. For an instant neither moved. Reid stiffened his knees and sidled toward them, wondering if he could get in under that blade. The Hun lowered it. "We . . . swore . . . an oath," he said thickly.

Erissa's own stance, of one ready to sidestep horns, eased a trifle. "I had to stop you," she said. "I told you, no needless killing. If nothing else, mightn't the traces of it bring alarm too soon? Cut strips from his loincloth and secure him. Duncan, can you find your garments without a lamp?"

Reid nodded. Light would drift through his open door. Uldin spat on the fallen man. "Very well," the Hun said. "But remember, Erissa, you're not my chief. I swore only to stand by you." He fleered at them both. "And, yes, now you have your Duncan, I no longer play stallion to your mare."

She gasped. Reid went quickly back to his chamber. Fumbling in the half-illumination, he put on one of the Cretan outfits, boots, puttees, kilt, and cap given him here. Over it he threw his Achaean tunic and cloak.

Erissa entered. He could barely see how her head drooped. "Duncan," she whispered, "I had to come. By whatever way."

"Of course." They stole a kiss. Meanwhile he thought: I'll see her young self.

Uldin was dragging the unconscious guard into a room when they emerged. Reid stopped in midstride. "Hurry," Erissa said.

"Could we take him along?" Reid asked. The other two stared. "I mean," he faltered, "he's a good man and . . . has a small daughter. . . . No, I suppose not."

They went out as the rescuers had come, by a side door giving on a wide staircase. Sphinxes flanked it, white under that low moon which frosted the descending garden terraces and the distant heights. In between, the bay was bridged by light that passed near the mountain's foot. The Great Bear stood in the north, and Polaris, but that was not the lodestar in this age. The air was warm and unmoving, filled by scents of new growth and chirring of crickets.

Reid could guess how entry was forced. The temple's men had never looked for attack. At night they posted one of their number in the corridor in sight of Reid's quarters. Should trouble arise, he could wrestle with the prisoner till his shouts fetched reinforcement from the inner building. Erissa simply opened this unbarred door, peeked through, and called him to her. She knew the layout, the procedure, and the words to disarm suspicion. When Velas got close, Uldin rushed from behind her.

She blew out the lamp, which had obviously been burning in the hall. (Velas would have carried it with him. She'd doubtless snatched it before it dropped from his grasp to the floor and shattered. How many would have had the thought or the quickness?) "Follow," she said. He expected her to take his hand, but she merely led the way. Uldin pushed Reid after her and took the rearguard. They shuffled down half-seen paths until they reached shore: not the dock, but a small beach where a boat lay grounded.

"Shove us off, Uldin," Erissa murmured. "Duncan, can you help me row? He catches too many crabs, makes too much noise." So she must have brought the craft in alone, the last several hundred yards or more.

The Hun also made a clatter getting around the dismounted mast and yard, and Reid's stomach twinged. But nobody called, nobody stirred; in holy peace, the Goddess' isle still slept. Very faintly, oars creaked in tholes and blades dripped. "Mid-bay," Erissa told Uldin, who sat silhouetted in the sternsheets as quartermaster.

When they rested, becalmed under moon and mountain on glass-dark water, Erissa said, "Duncan, this whole winter—" and moved over against him. He thought . . . he had too many thoughts whirling together . . . he made himself know what she had endured for his sake, and was as kind as he was able.

The embrace didn't take long. Uldin hawked. Erissa disengaged herself. "We'd best plan," she said unevenly.

"Uh, l-l-let's exchange information," stumbled out of Reid. "What's happened?"

In short harsh sentences, she told him. At the end, she said, "We docked today. Uldin stayed in the boat. If noticed, he'd be taken for an outland slave whose foot must not touch Atlantean soil. Otherwise there could have been questions. I took ashore a tale of distress and a bracelet to trade for respectable clothes." (Reid remembered anew that this was a world without coinage—bars of metal were the nearest thing to a standard medium of exchange, and none too commonly used—and he wondered belatedly if that was what he should have introduced.) "I witnessed the dancing." He had seldom heard such pain in so quiet a voice. She swallowed and continued: "In the merrymaking afterward, folk mingling freely in streets and inns, I had no trouble finding out what had become of you. Or what they were told had become of you. That story about your meditating was flat-clearly a lie. Knowing you were in the temple, I knew what part it had to be and how best to get there when everyone had gone to sleep. On the water, I changed back to this garb to spare the good that will be needed later. And we fetched you."

"I couldn't have done the same," he mumbled. "Instead, I'm the fool who let out the secret." He was glad his back was to the moon while he related.

In the end, she caught his hands. "Duncan, it was destined. And how could you have known? I, I should have foreseen, should have thought to warn—to find a way for us to flee Athens before—"

"Rein in," Uldin said. "What'll we do now?"

"Go on to Crete," Erissa replied. "I can find my parents' house, where I . . . will be dwelling. And my father had . . . has the ear of a palace councilor or two."

Cold moved down from Reid's scalp along his backbone and out to his fingertips. "No, wait," he said.

The idea had burst upon him. "We'd take days to cross the channel in this boat, and we'd arrive beggarly," he explained. "But yonder's the new warship. And the crew. I know where every member lives. They've no reason not to trust me. That ship will speak for us, and, and maybe it'll fight for Keft— Fast!" His oar smacked into the lagoon.

Erissa's followed. She matched him stroke for stroke. Presently his arms ached and his wind grew short. "How shall they leave without the temple stopping them?" she asked.

"We must be seaborne before the temple suspects anything," Reid panted. "Let me think." After a minute: "Yes. One lad can carry word to two more, who each tell two more, and so on. They'll obey, at least to the extent of meeting at the wharf. And the first I have in mind will follow us anywhere we say, over worldedge if need be. Dagonas—"

He stopped. Erissa had missed a stroke.

She resumed in a moment. "Dagonas," she said, and that was all.

"How'll we proceed?" Uldin asked. Reid told them.

They tied up alongside the rammer and scrambled ashore. Nobody else seemed awake. Houses were pale beneath the moon, streets guts of blackness. Dogs howled. The uphill run soon had Reid staggering, fire in his lungs. But he wasn't about to collapse before Erissa and . . . that swine Uldin. . . . "Here." He leaned against the adobe wall, shivering, head awhirl. Uldin pounded on the door for what seemed a long while.

It creaked open at last. A household servant blinked sleepily, lamp in hand. Reid had gotten back some strength. "Quick," he exclaimed. "I must see your master. And the young master. At once. Life and death."

She recognized him. He wondered what was in his expression to make her quail. She couldn't have seen Uldin or Erissa as more than shadows. "Yes, sir, yes, sir. Please come in. I'll call them."

She led the way to the atrium. "Please wait here, sirs, my lady." The chamber was well furnished; this was a rich family. A fresco of cranes in flight made vivid one wall; by another, a candle burned before the shrine of the Goddess. Erissa stood for a bit while Reid paced and Uldin squatted. Then, slowly, she knelt to the image. Her hands were pressed together so tightly that, however uncertain this light, Reid could see how the blood was driven from the nails.

The appearance of Dagonas and his father brought her to her feet. Perhaps only Reid noticed how the breath went ragged in her throat or how red and white ebbed across her face. Otherwise she stayed motionless and expressionless. Dagonas looked at her, and away, and back again. Puzzlement drew a slight crease between his large dark eyes, under his tumbled dark bangs.

"My lord Duncan." The father bowed. "You honor our house. But what brings you here at so strange an hour?"

"A stranger reason, and terrible," Reid answered. "Tonight the Goddess sent these twain, who made fully clear to me what those dreams mean that have been their forerunners."

He invented most of the story as he went along. The truth would have spilled more time than he, than anyone could afford. Erissa, a Keftiu lady resident in Mycenae, and Uldin, a trader from the Black Sea who had come to Tiryns, had likewise had troublous dreams. They sought the same oracle, which commanded them both to go to Atlantis and warn the foreigner in the temple to heed his own visions. As further evidence of wrath to come, they were told that they would witness a human sacrifice during the journey. This they took to be the shipwreck of the vessel they were on, from which they alone escaped. An Achaean fisherman on the island to which they swam carried them here in his boat—miracle in itself—but said he ought not to land on the holy isle; and when they brought Reid back, the fisherman was gone.

There could be no delay. Every person with any real civil or religious authority was in Knossos. Reid must bring his warning to them and to the Minos as fast as possible. Never mind what the Ariadne had decreed. Let the new galley be manned and provisioned and depart at once.

For the dream was that Atlantis would soon sink, in fire and wild waters. Let its people break off their feasting, let them take every boat to sea and wait. Else they would join those sailors that the angry gods had already drowned.

"I—" The older man shook his head, stunned. "I know not what to believe."

"Nor did I, until this final sign came to me," Reid replied.

He had fabled and talked mechanically, his consciousness wandering; for he *knew* he would reach Knossos where the girl awaited him. Now his mind came back. The man and boy, aroused wife and children and servants who stood fearfully in the door, became real; they could love and mourn and die. He said to Dagonas, "Crete will suffer wide destruction too. Won't you help me rescue Erissa?"

"Oh, yes, oh, yes." The boy started off at a trot which quickened toward a run.

His father's voice stopped him: "Wait! Let me think—"

"I cannot linger," Dagonas answered. He did briefly, though, gazing at Erissa. "You look like her," he said.

"We are kin." Her tone was faint. "Go."

The ship could not start before there was adequate light to steer by. But it took that long to gather crew and supplies anyway. The food came from their homes, water from the public cisterns, by Reid's command; he didn't dare try dealing with officialdom. As was, he sweated while his boys hastened down the streets—torch in one hand, since the moon had descended behind the western hills, streaming like a red comet's tail; bucket or bundle in the other, or tucked beneath the arm or slung across the shoulder—and thudded up the gangplank. Their families began to appear on the docks, an eddying of bodies in the gloom, an uneasy rustle of voices which rose and rose as questions received a grisly answer. This brought other, nearby householders forth. But most doors stayed shut. Folk slept well between their days of revelry.

Some decided to evacuate immediately. No few boats left, even before the galley did. Dagonas' parents were not included. They meant to carry the news from home to home till the corrida started and later ask that a public announcement be made. The assault on Velas, when news of that got about, wouldn't help; nor would offended lords spiritual and temporal who had not been consulted. But maybe the example of the hundred or so persons who were already afloat would inspire—maybe, maybe—

We've done what we can here, Reid thought. We'll keep trying elsewhere. Sixty miles or thereabouts to cross, and we average three or four knots. The boat from Athens that we're towing for insurance cuts that down a bit, but no matter, because we'll arrive by night in any case and have to lie out till dawn.

The east was paling. The ship's crew cast off and stood to their posts. The sight of Dagonas' father and mother, holding hands and waving, stayed with Reid until the thought came: In twenty-four hours, I'll see Erissa.

She did not seek him until well after sunrise. He stood in the bows of the upper deck. The morning lay around them, infinitely blue: cloudless overhead, surging beneath in fluid sapphires, cobalts, amethysts, turquoises and in snowy lacework. A favoring wind heeled the ship over a little; the planks moved like the back of a galloping animal. Bow waves hissed, rigging creaked and whistled. The sun was shaded off by the bellying genoa, but elsewhere made sparks and shimmers and called forth the first pungency of tar. A pair of dolphins played tag with the hull. Their torpedo bodies would rush in until it seemed a collision was certain, then veer off, graceful as a bull dancer. Gulls mewed above the masts.

Forward, a barely visible haziness betokened Crete. Aft, the cone of Pillar Mountain was a black blot on the horizon, the last glimpse of Atlantis.

"Duncan."

He turned. Like him, she had resumed Cretan garb. Her hair rippled in the breeze that felt cool on his own bare breast. Suddenly the crew, taking their ease on the thwarts below, and the helmsman and the two lookouts above, were far away.

"May I be here with you?" she asked.

"O gods, Erissa." He pulled her close. They didn't kiss, but she laid her cheek against his.

"I've wanted you so," she whispered.

He had no answer.

She released him. They stood side by side at the rail. "Eldritch to ride again on this ship," she said. "After all the years. I do not know if it is the ghost or I am."

"Reaching Knossos will be hard for you," he said, looking out to sea.

"Yes. My parents, their household . . . we had a pet monkey I called Mischief. . . . Well, it must be. And I will have been given to meet my dead once more. A-a-am I not favored?" She rubbed her eyes.

"Yourself," he said.

"That!" She caught his arm in both hands and leaned close to him. "Duncan, do you believe . . . can you imagine I'm jealous? I feared what you would think of me, old me. But to lie awake in my father's house, knowing that then, then I am having the dearest hours of my life—"

The mountain sundered.

# SEVENTEEN

Reid's first warning was a yell from a lookout. He snapped his head around. The cone no longer thrust out of the sea. In its place, monstrously swelling, was a wall of night.

An instant later the first shock wave struck. A fist hit Reid's whole body and smashed him down on the deck. The ship staggered, bow shoved into the water, which cataracted aboard. The roaring was so huge that it ceased to be sound, it became the universe, and the universe was a hammer.

The galley righted itself but reeled. Still the blackness grew. It filled half the circle of the world. It spread swiftly across the sky; for a while the sun shone ember red, then went out. Through and through the murk flared lightning, immense jags and sheets of it, hellish blue-white. Their thunders rolled amidst the steady bone-rattling bellow from Atlantis.

Reid glimpsed a stone, larger than the ship, glow as it fell from heaven. Blindly, he clutched the rail with one hand, Erissa with the other. The boulder struck half a mile off. Water reached for the zenith. White across black, lightning-lit, it did not splash under that impact, it shattered. A rising wind rived glasslike shards off it. It tumbled, and the sea was aboil. Reid saw the front wave rush upon them. Higher than the mastheads, fanged with spume, it made a noise of its own, a freight train rumble. He shouted, "Head 'er into that! Bow on or we're done!" The roaring, booming, whining, skirling gulped his voice and spat it back. For an idiotic instant he knew that he had cried in English.

But the quartermaster understood. He put the helm down and the galley, rocking, sluggish from bilges full, came around in time. Barely in time. Water torrented. Blind, beaten, Reid clung while the billow went over him. He had a moment to think: If we're not swept away, we'll drown here. I'm out of air, my ribs are being crushed— The galley wallowed. A mast lay in wreckage. The next wave took the next mast.

Lesser blocks were striking everywhere around. They made the sea explode in gouts of steam. One smote the deck and went bouncing down the length of the hull, leaving char marks where it touched. The boy at the helm screamed—he could not be heard, but lightning brought him out of the night, mouth open, eyelids stretched, free hand lifted in defense or appeal—until it reached him. He exploded too. Another wave washed the place clean where he had been.

The lookouts were likewise gone. Reid let go his hold and crawled aft. Somebody had to take the rudder. Erissa vaulted to the rowers' level, where they hung on and wailed. He glimpsed her, waist deep, slapping, scratching, forcing them to take oars and bailing buckets. But he didn't see much more; the tiller fought so crazily.

A second volcanic burst smote the air. A third. He was too stunned to count them, to know anything except that he must keep the prow into the waves. A couple of crewmen reached the deck, bearing axes. They cleared the broken masts away. Oars out, the galley had some power now to save itself; and the heaviness departed as the hull was emptied.

The seas ran black under the black sky, save when lightning turned them into brass. Then each drop flung off their crests stood livid, as if frozen in flight. Thunder banged through the ongoing growl and rush and shriek, and blindness clapped back down again. The air reeked of brimstone and poison.

Ash began to fall. Rain followed, driven by the wind till it hit like spears; but it was not clean water, it was gritty, lacerating mud. A new bang and drumfire betokened a new eruption. They were fainter this time than the storm noises.

Erissa returned, chinning herself to the upper deck since the ladders were smashed. Reid couldn't see her till she was close; he could see almost nothing through the ashen acid rain; the bows were invisible, he steered by feel and by the occasional glimpse when some fulguration was fierce enough to penetrate the darkness and flog his eardrums with its thunder. She had lost her skirt, shed her sandals, was nude except for the hair and dust plastered to her skin. She laid her hand over his on the tiller, her lips to his ear. He could barely hear her: "Let me help you."

"Thanks." He didn't need it physically. The ship was under control and the weather couldn't get worse than a hurricane. But it was good to have her beside him on this deck that lurched through ruin.

*Crack!* flared a lightning bolt. He glimpsed her profile etched white athwart the horrible sky. She looked at him, and bow-ward again, showing no more than the will to stay afloat. Darkness fell anew, and wind-yell and wave-rush; thunder rolled like the wheels of an Achaean war chariot.

The hours passed.

When Crete hove in view, it was sudden. There the cliffs were, stark above a rage of surf. Reid slammed the helm over. Erissa, leaning beside him—for once more the rudder sought to wrench free and thresh among murderous currents—exclaimed, "It can't be this soon!" Her voice was blown thin and tattered through the clamor, the boom, the hiss of black rain.

"We were carried on a tsunami," he called in reply, but doubted if she heard. Never mind. The need was to claw off that shore. The torrents which had already scarred the heights and borne away who knew how many homes and dwellers were trying to fling this vessel on the rocks. By another flash, Reid saw the wreck of another galley, high up on ground stripped bare.

Atlantis had sunk. He hoped fleetingly that Velas' little girl had been killed at once, by the initial blast, before she had time to cry for her daddy. The sea power of the Minos was shattered. Theseus and his merry men were overrunning what remained of quake-tumbled Knossos. Reid wondered dimly, through aches and exhaustion, what reason was left to strive.

Well, whatever Erissa, who had now twice in her life lost the life of her people, waged war for. Maybe just pride, he thought in his battered head: to scorn death's warm temptation, to fight on after Ragnarok.

They seemed to have won clear. He left her at the tiller and went below to check on his crew. Eight had been lost overboard, besides the boy who saw a red-hot stone coming for him. Several more had collapsed, lay rolling between the benches. The rest rowed or bailed, automatons, emptiness behind their eyes. Uldin huddled in the bilge, face covered by arms against the lightning that streaked over him. When Reid shook the Hun, he retched.

Well, Reid thought dully, we'll get a safe distance out, make a sea anchor from a sail and spar if the towed boat doesn't suffice, and rest. To sleep, perchance to dream—what dreams may come?

Smoke still sooted heaven, but the sun's ball, the color of half-clotted blood, rolled westward in it. Crete could be seen as a blurry mass at the gray-brown edge of vision. The wind had dropped for a while, the rain had ceased, the air lay thick and stinking. Waves chopped the galley in a whoosh and squelp, left it to rock and swing while they trundled onward. The waters were dark, sludgy, corrupted with cinders.

Northward, where Atlantis had been, total blackness reared nightmare huge. Lightning scribbled swift symbols across it, but at this distance the thunders came only as a continued muttering.

They sat gathered on the top deck: forty-one young Minoans, naked or nearly so, slumped over their knees, grimed, bleeding from gale-blown grit, hollowed out less by fatigue—a few hours' ease restored those bodies to tautness—than by that which had slain their Atlantis. Uldin squatted among them, flinching at each far-off blink and bang but his scarred features truculently set. Erect to confront them, dressed in sodden Achaean tunics, were Reid and Erissa.

The American dragged the words out of himself: "We had a forevision of the destruction of your homeland and Keft's conquest by barbarians. We tried to give warning to your folk and to the Minos. But unless those boats which left when we did weathered the storm, we failed altogether. Now what should we do?"

"What's left?" a boy asked through tears.

"Life," Erissa told him.

"We . . . could seek Athens," Uldin said. "In spite of everything—"

Dagonas sprang up and struck him across the mouth. He rose too, cursing, and drew his saber. Knives flew free of sailors' belts. Erissa leaped. She caught Uldin's sword arm and clung. "Stop!" she shouted. "Blood brotherhood!"

"Not with him," the Hun grated. Dagonas poised, knife in fist.

Erissa sneered: "Especially with him, who manned an oar while you cowered and yammered like a eunuch."

She released him. Uldin appeared to shrink into himself. He crept aside, hunkered down, and spoke no more.

Erissa returned to Reid. In the dull red-gray light, he saw that her nostrils flared and her head was carried high. "You shouldn't have," he stammered. "I—I was too slow, as always."

She swung upon the crew. "Never give in," she said. "Our colonies remain, on islands throughout these waters. They're shaken, but most of them will abide. If we no longer rule the whole sea, we can rule our own lives while they last. We'll seek a place—Rhodes would be best, I think—where we can start afresh. In the name of the Goddess!"

"That bitch who betrayed us?" answered the weeping boy.

Dagonas signed himself and gasped, "Be quiet! Do you want to bring down more wrath?"

"What worse can She do?" the boy said.

Erissa told them: "The law is that men must render account to the gods, but not the gods to men. I am not sure this is right. But it makes no difference. The Labyrinth has fallen. I will not forsake the Goddess in Her need."

Dagonas, who had remained standing, went to the rail and peered through the gloom toward Crete. "Then let's seek

Rhodes," he said. "But first—you have a namesake yonder, Erissa."

She nodded. "We have many dear ones there, and room and provisions. Do you think we might try to rescue some?"

"As many as may be," the young man said; and even in this sullen illumination, Reid saw how he flushed, "but before all, the girl Erissa."

The woman laid a hand on his shoulder and looked long into his face. "That's Dagonas who speaks," she said wonderingly.

Reid stirred. "You, uh, y-y-you think we can send a party ashore?" he stuttered.

"Yes," she answered with the calm that had been hers for most of these hours. "I know that headland, therefore I know we can reach Knossos harbor before nightfall. Whatever Theseus is doing, has done, most of the city must yet be in chaos. A band of men, armed and determined, should be able to make their way." The big eyes resting on him were the same clear green as would shine across this sea once more, come winter. "They will, you know."

He nodded. I can't lose, he thought, until after I have the girl back whose image dances among those funeral clouds. Later —well, later we'll be free of foreknowledge.

He did draw old Erissa aside and murmur to her, "You haven't any recollection, have you, of anyone on Rhodes this year who might have been yourself?"

"No," she said.

"But then—"

"Then I will most likely never come there alive," she said quietly. "Or something else may happen. Something else has in truth already happened, since the Knossos where I remember we had each other is no longer waiting for us. No matter now. Let's do what we can, first for that girl—" She paused. "Strange," she said, "to think of myself as a being in pain and need of help." Drawing breath: "First we do what we can for her and whoever else we can reach. Afterward we—you and I—maybe we can be happy, or maybe we can endure."

# EIGHTEEN

LITTLE REMAINED in the harbor: snags of buildings, fragments of ships, broken corpses, strewn goods, mud-filled streets. Downward-sifting dust had covered all bright walls with grayness. The sun smoldered barely above those heights where Knossos lay. There stood pillars of smoke. The city was burning.

Reid and Erissa took no more than half a dozen along in the boat. The dismasted galley needed oarsmen; why risk them ashore? A large party would draw attention, without being large enough to deal with the consequences. Besides Dagonas and Uldin, they had Ashkel, Tylisson, Haras, and Rhizon. There had been no chance to stow armor except for bucklers. Weapons were swords, knives, a couple of pikes. Reid gripped his spear convulsively. It was the sole instrument with which he might hope to do anything useful.

They moored at the stump of a pier and climbed over the wreckage. Tidal waves had left the ground soaked; muck lay ankle-deep on the lower levels, chilly, plopping and sucking around sandals. Dust filled the air, the nose, the mouth. Sweat, running down skin in the unnatural heat, made channels through that grime.

None greeted the landing. Doubtless Theseus would have the area occupied next morning in anticipation of his ships. At the moment, though, he must have everything he could do, bringing Knossos somewhat under control.

"He established himself—he will take what parts of the Labyrinth the quakes left standing," Erissa said. "The Minos he slew with his own hand, our gentle old Minos. His patrols ranged about through the night, disarming citizens, herding many together for slavery. Tomorrow he summoned his supporters among the folk. He made the bull sacrifice in token that now he was king. The Ariadne stood beside him. Thus I was told, years afterward, by people who were there. The knowledge may help us now."

"It makes no difference," Uldin grunted. "What else would you expect? We'll be avoiding patrols in any case."

"If one finds us," Dagonas grated, "the worse for it."

"We'll go to your home first," Reid suggested to Erissa, "and fetch the girl and as many more as we're able. From them we can perhaps get better information about what's going on. On the way back, we can try to rescue others."

That's the most we can do, he thought. Pick up some human pieces. But how can this be? She thought she and I—in her father's house, in a city still at peace—where will we, then? How? When? Could time really be changeable?

It better not be. If it is, we'll likely be discovered and killed. I'd never have dared this foray if I didn't believe it was fated that we rescue the dancer and afterward lose her.

He glanced at Erissa. In the failing light, silhouetted against a half crumbled wall, she went striding as if to her bulls. The cameo profile was held so steady that he could almost have called her expression serene. He thought: She would dare.

The road wound inland for a steep two or three miles. Above the reach of the tsunamis, most of the poplars that lined the way still stood, though some were uprooted and gale-broken boughs were strewn about. Behind these trees, on either side, had been the cottages of smallholders, the villas of the wealthy; but they lay in rubble. A stray cow wandered lowing—for her calf? Reid couldn't make out anything else. But dusk was upon him and vision didn't reach far.

It did find Knossos, whose death fleckered red and yellow across the clouds ahead. At last the fires themselves came into sight, scores leaping above a black jaggedness of cast-down walls. When a roof fell in, sparks spouted as if from a volcano. The roaring grew ever louder, the reek and sting of smoke sharper, as Reid's band trudged on.

Knossos had not been defended. What need had the sea king's people for fortifications ashore? Where a gate would elsewhere have risen, the road branched off in several wide, flagged streets. The city had been a larger version of Atlantis. Erissa pointed her spear down one of the avenues. "That way," she said tonelessly.

Full night had come. Reid groped along by flamelight, stumbling on fallen blocks and baulks, once in a while putting his foot on what he suddenly knew for a dead body. Through the crackling he heard occasional screams. He squinted into the roil of smoke but saw no one except a woman who sat in a doorway and rocked herself. She did not look back at him, she looked through him. The man beside her had been killed by a weapon. Soot and dust rained steadily upon her.

Dagonas stopped. "Quick! Aside!" he hissed. A second later they heard what his young ears had: tramping feet, clanking metal. Crouched in the shadows of a narrow side street, they saw an Achaean squad go past. Only two men were in the full gear—nodding plumes, shining helmets, blowing cloaks, armor, shields—that must have been smuggled along. The rest, numbering seven, were clad in ordinary wise and carried merely swords, pikes, axes, a sling. Two were Cretan.

"By Asterion—those traitors—!" Ashkel's blade caught the light in a gleam. Two comrades wrestled him to a halt before he could charge. The gang went past.

"We'll scarcely meet more," Erissa said. "Theseus doesn't have many here on his side. It's only that none are left to fight on ours. Those who might have rallied them, the nobles, were of course seized or slain immediately; and leaderless men can do nothing except run." She started off afresh.

They met more dead, more grieving. Hurt folk croaked for help, for water; hardest was the necessity to pass them by without answering. Or was the worst those glimpsed forms that scuttled out of sight—Cretans who feared this party was also among the looters, rapers, and slave takers?

When they came to a certain square, Erissa halted. "My home." Her voice was no longer entirely steady.

Most of the buildings around had escaped extreme damage. The wavering hazy light of a fire some distance off showed cracked façades, sagging doors, wall paintings blurred by dust; but they stood. On the one at which she pointed, Reid could just make out that there had been depicted, triumphal in a field of lilies, the bull dance.

She caught his hand. They crossed the plaza.

Night gaped in the house. After knocking with his spear butt, peering inside at stripped and tumbled emptiness, Reid said slowly: "I'm afraid no one's here. Looks as if it's been plundered. I suppose the folk fled."

"Where?" Dagonas' voice was raw.

"Oh, I can tell you, I can tell you, friends." The answer drifted from within. "Wait and I'll tell you. Shared sorrow is best."

The man who shuffled out was wrinkled, bald, blinking from half-blind eyes. Erissa choked, "Balon."

"Aye, aye, you know Balon, do you?" he said. "Old Balon, too old to be worth hauling off and selling—they pensioned him in this family, though, they did, because he worked faithfully over the years for a good master, yes, that I did. Why, the children used to come and beg me for a story. . . . All gone. All gone."

She dropped her spear and pulled him to her. "Balon, old dear," she said raggedly, "do you remember Erissa?"

"That I do, that I do, and will for what days remain to me. I hope he'll not be too unkind to her. She might charm her way into his graces, you know. She could charm the birds down out of the trees. But I don't know, I don't know. They said something about him and the Ariadne, when they came for her."

"For who?" Dagonas yelled.

"Why, Erissa. Right after the quake and the darkness and winds, almost. She'd been telling about this man she met on Atlantis—you could warm your hands at her happiness—and then the quake and— Her father's been ill, you know. Pains in the chest. Weak. He couldn't well move. So she stayed. Then, crash, there they were at the door. They'd been sent special. Theseus, they said, wanted Erissa. They wanted loot and slaves. They got both, after they'd bound my little Erissa who was going to win the garland and marry that foreign man she loved. But not old Balon. Nor his master. Master died, he did, right then and there, when that Achaean tramped into the bedroom and grabbed mistress—said she wouldn't fetch much but looked like she had a few years of grain-grinding in her—yes, master's dead in there. I laid him out. Now I'm waiting to follow him. I'd have followed the rest of the family, I begged they'd take me along, but the soldiers laughed. So all poor Balon can do is wait by master's bedside."

Erissa shook him. "Where are they?" she cried.

"Oh? Oh?" The servant squinted. "You look like her. You really do," he mumbled. "But you can't be kinfolk. Can you? I knew this whole house, I did. Every member, every cousin and nephew and baby in the Thalassocracy. They'd always tell old Balon the news when they came visiting here, and I'd always remember. . . . They're in some pen or other, I guess, under heavy guard. You'll not rescue them, I fear."

"Erissa!" Reid demanded. "Her too?"

"No. No. I told you. Didn't I? Something special about her. Theseus, our conqueror, that is, King Theseus wanted her special. He sent men after her right away, before she might escape. They'd had to fight on the way here, they told me; I saw blood on them; that's the kind of hurry they were in. I don't know why. The rest of the household, brothers, sisters, children, servants, they just collected incidental-like, along with the loot. Erissa was what they really came for. I suppose she's in the Labyrinth. Now can I go back to master?"

Mount Iouktas, where Asterion was buried, in whose cave shrine Lydra had had her vision, bulked ebon across the clouds. Approaching from above—the least unsafe, when every path was beset—Reid could make out the palace against the burning further down: cyclopean walls, high pillars, broad staircases, sprawling over acres, grand even when half shattered. A few watchfires glowed red in courtyards.

"We're out of our minds," Uldin grumbled. "Heading into a wolf's den, a maze where we could wander lost till dawn."

"Blood brotherhood," Erissa answered. Since Balon refused to seek the galley, she had masked herself; she moved with fluid swiftness as before, but face and voice might have belonged to brazen Talos whom legend said once guarded Crete. "I remember those halls. We should be able to get around in them better than the enemy."

"But for a single stupid wench—"

"Go back if you're afraid," Dagonas said scornfully.

"No, no, I come."

"If she's important to Theseus, she must be important to our side," Tylisson said. "Or at least we may kill a few Achaeans."

They continued their stealthy progress. Reid went in the van beside Erissa. He saw her only as a shadow and a spearhead; but bending close, touching the rough wool tunic, breathing a hint of her amidst fumes and cinders, he thought: She's here. She is. She's not the girl she was, but she's the woman that the girl became.

"Should we go through with this?" he whispered.

"We did," she replied.

"Did we? In just this way?"

"Yes. I know now what really happened tonight. If we fail our duty—why, maybe I'll never meet you again, Duncan. Maybe we'll never have had those moments that were ours."

"What about the risk to our friends?"

"They fight in their own people's cause. This hour is for more than you and me. Tylisson spoke well. Think. Why did Theseus want that girl so badly? Because she's full of strangeness; she's fated to return to herself. He—and Lydra, I suppose—dare not let an enemy of such unknown powers go loose. But having taken her, will they not use her? She's only a girl, Duncan. She can be broken to their will.

"The free Keftiu on the lesser islands could be overrun. But if this Chosen One escapes him, Theseus will be daunted. He'll stay his hand, rest content with uniting Attica, leave the Aegean Sea in peace." For an instant, malice spat: "Yes, he'll become so shy of the Goddess' faith that he'll not dare use it for his state-craft as he now plans to. He'll set the Ariadne off where she can do no more harm."

"Hsh," cautioned Uldin.

Down on their bellies, they crawled along garden walks. Through leaves, Reid saw the nearest of the campfires. It cast its glimmer around a courtyard, on a fallen pillar and a row of huge storage jars lined along the masonry. Two Achaeans sat drinking. A royal slave scuttled to keep their beakers full; for him life hadn't changed much. A third man must be on duty, because he was fully equipped and on his feet. The light flowed off his bronze. He laughed and jested with his companions, though. Reid caught a snatch: "—When the ships come tomorrow or next day, when we've ample men, that's when the roundup really begins and maybe you'll find that girl who got away, Hippomenes—" In a corner lay what the American thought were two asleep. He stole sufficiently close by to discover that they were Cretans. Festival wreaths were withering on their temples, above blank eyes and cut throats. Their blood had pooled widely before it clotted.

Hugging the wall, Erissa led her group to an unwatched side entrance. The first several yards of corridor beyond were tomb black. Then they emerged in another at right angles, where lamps burned at intervals. Between doorways romped a mural of bulls, dolphins, bees, gulls, blossoms, youths, maidens, everything that was glad. Erissa nodded. "I expected those lights," she said. "The Ariadne, if no one else, would direct the laying down of such a thread so the conquerors can find their way along the main halls."

Shadows bulked and slunk, demon-shaped; but the air was blessedly cool and clean. They moved toward that section Erissa believed was their likeliest goal. How full of life these corridors, these rooms must have been, one day ago. The passage wasn't straight, it wound, wildly intersected.

A voice beyond a corner stabbed at Reid. Theseus! "Well, that's done. I wasn't sure I could."

Lydra: "I told you my presence would ward you."

"Yes. I was listening to your prayers the whole while. Was I wrong to enjoy it? I did. More than I expected."

"You will not again, will you? Here I am."

"Enough."

Reid risked a peek. Yards off was a door where two full-equipped warriors stood guard, spears grounded, swords at waist, shields ashine in the lamplight. Theseus and Ariadne were departing in the opposite direction. The prince wore only a tunic and glaive; his yellow mane seemed brighter than the bronze, and he walked with the gait of one who has taken more than a kingdom. Lydra, in Cretan priestess garb, clung to his arm.

What's going on? Reid wondered icily.

"Hurry, we can kill them," Ashkel breathed.

"No, that's Theseus himself," Erissa answered. "More men are sure to be in call."

"To die killing Theseus—" Rhizon's blade lifted.

"Hold. We're here to save the maiden," Dagonas answered. "Let him take the soldiers waiting for him out of earshot."

They stood. Hearts thuttered.

"Go!" Erissa commanded.

Reid led the charge around the corner. An Achaean yelled and cast his spear. Haras took it in the stomach. He fell, spouting blood, fighting not to scream. Reid glimpsed the gray beardless face and thought—events seemed to be happening very slowly; there was ample time to think—Merciful. A major artery was cut, I guess. Otherwise he'd have had to die of peritonitis, by stages.

The second man prodded with his pike. Reid wielded his own clumsily, like a club, trying to knock aside the point that lunged at him. Wood clattered. Erissa caught the shaft and hung on. The Athenian let go and drew his sword. Tylisson rushed.

With a slight movement of shield, the Athenian sent the Cretan blade gliding off it. His own thrust over the top. Tylisson staggered back, clutching a lacerated arm. "Help! To aid, to aid!" the sentries were bawling.

Uldin attacked one. His saber whined and belled. When the bronze stabbed at him, he wasn't there; he bounced from side to side. Fighting, he screamed. The noise clawed. Rhizon dodged in and flung both arms around the shield, pulling it down. Uldin laughed and swung. The Achaean's head bounced free. It lay there staring at its body. Blood soaked its long hair. Probably some woman and children at home were going to miss it.

Dagonas had been keeping the other man busy. Now Uldin, Ashkel, and Rhizon could join him. The Achaean backed off, working with shield and sword. Metal clashed; lungs rasped. The door was undefended.

Reid tried it. The latch had been left off. Opening, he stepped into a chamber that must be a shrine. Life-size in ivory, gold, and silver, the Goddess held out her snakes who were the beloved dead. Behind her was painted the sun bull Asterion, to right the octopus which meant admiralty, to left the wheat sheaf which meant peace and harvest. A single lamp burned before the altar. Young Erissa knelt nearby; but she faced away, sagging, countenance hidden by the loose dark hair. Beneath her was the full skirt of festival, torn off by the hands which later bruised her breasts.

"Erissa." Reid lurched toward the shape.

Her older self brushed past him, bent down, laid arms around the girl. In the young face next to the half-aged one, Reid saw the same emptiness which had been in his men after Atlantis was whelmed. She stared and did not know him.

"What's happened?" he begged.

The woman said: "What do you think? Her destiny was supposed to lie with you. Her consecration lay in her being a maiden. Theseus feared them both. So he took them away. I daresay Lydra counseled him to it. We know she helped."

Reid thought dully: Sure, her first son was fathered by a tall blond man.

A yell and clangor outside spelled the end of combat. Erissa held Erissa and said most gently, "Come, let's be gone. I can heal part of your hurt, child." More noise broke loose. The garrison elsewhere had heard the fighting.

Reid glanced out. The second sentry lay slain across the body of Haras. But down the hall came a dozen warriors; and none of this party had armor, and Tylisson was disabled.

Dagonas sped to the doorway. "Get out," he panted. "We can hold them a while. Get her down to the ship."

Uldin spat. "Go with them, Cretan," he said. "The lot of you. You'll need what strength you have. I'll keep the corridor."

Erissa of the white lock, upbearing the girl who followed along like a sleepwalker, said, "That's much to ask."

The Athenians stood hesitant, mustering their nerve to attack. They must have heard rumors. Yes, Reid knew: for the sake of what Keftiu remain, she who danced with the bulls and is even now a vessel of Power cannot be let fall back into the hands of their lord.

They were no cowards. In a minute they'd advance.

Uldin spat again. "A Hun and a dozen waddling charioteers. Good odds." His gaze came to rest on the woman. "I could wish to die on a steppe where cornflowers bloom, in sunlight, a horse beneath me," he said. "But you kept your side of our bargain. Farewell."

He had taken a shield. Now he planted himself in the middle of the hall, saber aloft. "What're you waiting for?" he called, and added a volley of obscene taunts.

Erissa plucked Reid's tunic. "Come," she said.

That departure shocked the Athenians into motion. They advanced four abreast. Those behind the front rank wielded spears. Uldin let them get near. Abruptly he squatted, shield over his head, and smote at a leg where flesh showed between greave and kilt. The man clattered down, yammering. Uldin had already whirled and wounded another. Blades clashed on his defense.

He sprang from his crouch, straight at a third man, who fell against his neighbor. They tumbled, and Uldin's sword went *snick-snick*. A spear pierced him. He didn't seem to notice. Forcing his way into the mass of them, he cut right and left. They piled on him at last, but nonetheless they needed a goodly while to end the battle, and no survivor among them was ever quite hale again.

The galley stood out to sea. It had a number of refugees aboard, those on whom Reid's party had chanced. There'd been no time to look around for more, though. The hue and cry were out. A patrol found them near the docks, and it became a running fight—hit, take a blow, grope onward in the dark—until they got to their boat. At that point they made a stand and kept the Achaeans busy until reinforcements had been ferried from the ship and a hopelessly outnumbered enemy was ground into meat. Reid was too numb to regret that. And it was necessary, he realized, if the Knossians were to be rowed to safety.

Once in open water they could rest. No other vessel was left afloat near the sea king's home. Exhausted, they lay to.

Wind was slowly rising afresh. By morning it would whip the fires in the city to a conflagration whose traces would remain when the ruins were dug up more than three thousand years hence. The next days would see many storms as the troubled atmosphere cleansed itself. But the ship could ride unattended till dawn. Reid would be the lookout. He wasn't going to get to sleep anyway, he knew.

He stood in the bows on the upper deck, where he and Erissa had been that morning. (Only that morning? Less than a single turn of the planet?) Aft, the dim forms of crew and fugitives stirred, mumbled, uneasily asleep. The hull rocked under always heavier, noisier blows. The wind whittered hot from the south. It still carried needles of volcanic ash—tossed back and forth between Greece and Egypt till finally they came to rest—but smelled less evil than before.

Shielded by a strung scrap of sailcloth, a candle burned. Young

Erissa lay on a straw pallet. Her older self had put clothes on her. She looked upward, but he couldn't tell if she really saw. Her features were slumbrous. The woman knelt over her, hair and cloak tossing in the gusts, and crooned, "Rest, rest, rest. All is well, my darling. We'll care for you. We love you."

"Duncan," said the half parted lips, which had been like flower petals but were puffed and broken from the blow of a fist.

"Here is Duncan." The woman beckoned. Reid could but obey. How deny Erissa the creation of that which would keep her alive through the years to come?

Strange, though, to hear her tell of days and nights which had never been and would never be. Maybe it was best this way. Nothing real could be so beautiful.

Dagonas must not know the truth, and wouldn't. Erissa would speak little about it. He'd assume that tonight she had merely been struck, and earlier on Atlantis she and the god called Duncan—

The first light of dawn sneaked through scudding ash-clouds. Erissa left peace upon the girl's slumbering countenance, rose, and said out of her own haggardness: "We're not free yet."

"What?" He blinked. His lids felt sandy as the wind. His being creaked with weariness.

"She and Dagonas have to go off in our boat, you know," the woman said. "Otherwise Theseus might still find and use her. After that, we've paid our ransom." She pointed. "Look."

His gaze followed her arm, past the steeps of Crete on the horizon, across the sea which roiled black, west to that corner of the world whence the Achaean galleys came striding. At their head was a giant which could only be the work of Oleg.

# NINETEEN

THE RUSSIAN had built the closest possible copy of a Byzantine capital ship in his own century. Twice as long and thrice as high as Reid's, it had two lateen-rigged masts; but today, with the wind foul, it went on a hundred double-banked oars. Its beak tore the waves as if they were enemy hulls. Decked fore and aft, it bore equally outsize catapults. Amidships a pair of booms extended, great boulders suspended at their ends for dropping on hostile crews. Shields were hung on frames at the waist, where the gunwale dropped low, to protect the rowers. Above those benches swarmed warriors.

"Alert!" Reid yelled. "Wake, wake!"

His folk dragged themselves from sleep. Dagonas alone seemed to have kept vitality. He bounded to Reid and the Erissas. "What'll we do?" he cried. "They're fresh, those dogs. They can raise sail if they choose. We'll never outrun them. And when we're caught—" He stared down at the girl and groaned.

"We head for the big vessel," Reid told him. "Its captain is my friend, who won't knowingly fight against us. I hope."

The woman bit her lip. "You youngsters—Well, we must see. Stay close by her, Dagonas."

She drew Reid aside. "Something will go wrong," she said bleakly.

"I'm afraid so," he agreed. "But we've no choice, have we? And . . . remember our hope. That time travelers, hovering somewhere about, will notice a ship that doesn't belong in this age and come for a closer inspection. Well, here we have two. His is even more out of place than ours. We *must* get together with him."

He cast a glance upward but saw only clouds, gray, brown, and black, piling southward into lightning-shot masses that betokened a new storm. Of course, futurian observers might well have some device for invisibility.

"If we're not rescued—" he began, and faltered.

"Then we make our way together." Both their gazes strayed to the couple in the bows, the sleeping, smiling girl and the boy who crouched before her. "Or we die," Erissa finished. "But those two will live. In the long run, I've been lucky. I pray that you have been too."

The oars ground into motion. It was necessary to intercept the dromon before a lesser galley cut this one off. The Achaeans were widely strewn, in no particular formation—the idea of a real navy would not occur for centuries, now that the only one in the world was gone—but they were bound to notice the peculiar vessel and its obviously Minoan markings. Closing in, they would see that the people aboard were Keftiu, fair game.

The deck rolled. Waves splashed over the rails onto near-naked lads, who rowing must push aside bewildered men, huddled women, wailing children. Wind shrilled and carried the remote sound of thunder.

"You're not afraid, Duncan, are you?" Erissa asked.

"No," he said, and was faintly surprised to note that that was true. He thought: Maybe I've learned courage from her.

The dromon changed course. Evidently its captain was himself interested in contact. They were gesturing and hailing on that foredeck, but their voices blew away and as yet no individuals were recognizable.

However— "My God!" exploded from Reid. "They're loading the catapults!"

"That's our disaster, then," Erissa said between clenched teeth. "They've seen our ram and are afraid."

A ball of flame, tow soaked in pitch and set ablaze, arced from the Athenian. Reid thought wildly: Must be the closest Oleg could come to Greek fire. "Forward!" he shouted. "We've got to close in—show him who we are—"

The first two missiles hissed into the sea. The third smote the upper deck. No persons remained there except Reid's party and the helmsman. The latter yelled and sprang below. Reid couldn't blame him much. These tarred and seasoned planks were a tinderbox. Flames gushed. The American jumped down likewise, into chaos. "Row on, row on!" he bawled. "And somebody help me!" He grabbed a bailing bucket, filled it over the side, handed it up to Erissa the woman.

She cast the water across the fire but called, "No use. Another has hit. The wind's fanning them."

"Well, get the young ones to the boat!"

"Aye. Erissa, awake. You, Dagonas, follow me."

They joined Reid in the stern. Amidst rampant confusion, only a couple of men noticed him draw the lifeboat in. Tylisson pushed close and said through the racket, "No room for more than a few in that, skipper."

Reid nodded. "Only these two will go," he said, pointing.

"Me, desert you?" Dagonas protested.

Reid met his eyes. "You're not doing that," he said. "You're serving better than you'll ever know." His right hand gripped the boy's. His left arm went around the shoulders of the girl, who was coming out of her drowse into bewildered and terrified awareness. Overhead, the upper deck roared with its burning. Forward, folk crouched and wailed.

"Erissa," he said to her, "go. Endure. Know that in the end I'll call you back to me." He could merely kiss her on the brow. "Dagonas, never leave her. Farewell."

The woman briefly embraced her and the lad. They entered the boat. Dagonas stayed troubled at the idea of taking none else along. But before he could speak further, Reid slipped the tow line. Shoved by wind and wave, the craft fell quickly astern. It looked terribly frail and alone. Dagonas worked to step the mast. Before long, smoke off the blazing deck hid him and young Erissa from sight.

"You're the captain," Tylisson said, "but may I ask why you let no others go free?"

"I have my reasons," the American answered. He didn't give his main one: that whoever might have traveled off was probably better dead than doomed to a slavery from which only the boldest could escape.

The woman said, in a strange tone, "Now we are free."

Reid thought: Free to die. We didn't send those kids off just to play out a last act that is also the first, nor even to keep them from becoming the talismans which give the barbarians the will to overrun what's left of civilization. We sent them off to make certain they'll live. This ship is done for, and most likely we are ourselves. But I too will keep striving, Erissa.

"Come," he ordered Tylisson. "Help me bring that panic under control."

Shouting, cuffing, kicking, they restored a measure of discipline. The Knossians crowded on the midthwarts, the Atlanteans took up oars which, secured by thongs, had not come adrift. The burning vessel picked up new headway.

"Let's go into the bows and show ourselves," Reid said to Erissa.

They were now not far from the dromon. Across the blustery space between, blurred by smoke and spindrift, they could make out faces. Diores, yes, on the foredeck, overseeing a catapult gang; and Oleg, by God, Oleg standing big and byrnied near him. Reid sprang onto the prow rail and clung to the stempost. Heat gnawed at him from the fire behind. "Oleg!" he yelled. "Don't you know us?"

"*Bozhe moi!*" the Russian bawled back. "Duncan, Erissa—I wondered—hold off, fellows! Get a boat over there!"

Reid saw Diores shake his head. He could imagine the admiral's words: "Too dangerous, them. Better we finish them while we can."

Oleg roared indignation and lifted his ax. Diores snapped a word. A pair of warriors moved to arrest Oleg. His ax whistled. They retreated. Diores called to the rest.

"Hang on, we're coming!" Reid shouted. Down the length of the hull, to his rowers and to Ashkel at the steering oar which had been improvised to replace the tiller: "Our last chance. To disable that monster, board, seize their boats!"

Hoarse howls answered him. Muscles writhed under sooty, sweat-smeared skins. The galley plunged ahead. Reid pulled Erissa back to safety.

Oleg, on the dromon, had fought his way to Diores. The Athenian drew blade and lunged at him. Oleg's ax knocked the sword free. A second, sidewise blow across the breastplate sent Diores over the side. Cased in bronze, he sank when he struck. Oleg whirled to confront the warriors.

The lesser ship rammed, in a dreadful snapping of oars. Its beak sheared into planks. The fire upon it clutched at the hull and rigging of the dromon. Reid seized a grapnel, swung it around his head, hooked a rail and went up the rope hand over hand. The thought flitted through him: So both these anachronisms are finished. Nobody's going to build more in this generation . . . not till long afterward, when Achaeans, Argives, Danaans, Dorians have become Greeks and the blood of the old Keftiu seafarers runs in all their veins—

A shining shape descended from the clouds.

# TWENTY

THE DARK, kindly man had said:

"No, we did not know about you. Our record of your being cast away here-now and eventually rescued lies in our own future, you see. Time expeditions being so limited in number, none are wasted on doubling back into the near past. But your conjecture was right that observers would be sent to the catastrophe—a geologically almost unique event—and its immediate aftermath. Likewise was your hope that we would notice those outlandish vessels and guess what must have happened. Therefore, do not feel that you have gone through a puppet routine. You survived, in the end you delivered yourselves, by your own efforts. Weaklings would have perished, fools would have stayed marooned.

"No, we regret the infeasibility of searching for that lifeboat. The region is too large and stormy, our capability too limited. And when everything is reckoned together, good as well as ill: if it were possible, would you want to lose your past? Out of it must come your tomorrows.

"We have taken your Atlantean and Knossian friends back to Crete, to the hinterland where the conquerors will not soon arrive. Their memories of the previous day have been blanked. The suggestion has been planted that they, fleeing, were wrecked. This is only to spare them needless doubts and terrors that would handicap them in rebuilding their lives. Again, you castaways have honor, for you were the means of their saving, and of the fact that archeologists will not find many bones under the Santorini lava.

"The enemy crew? They saw little; you recall that we rendered everyone aboard unconscious as we approached. Their Achaean identity being obvious, we left them to awaken in a few minutes and be taken off by another ship before theirs sank.

"Still, enough had been seen by the fleet—an apparition of angry gods—that Theseus on his return cast the *mentatór* into the sea. That is desirable. Still more desirable is the chastening you gave him when you pulled free from the teeth of his victory that girl in whom he believed he had triumphed even over the Goddess. Be consoled by the knowledge that now he will not simply spare the Cretan island colonies; he will on the whole become a good king, and the Mycenaean civilization will be a worthy child of the Minoan and a leaven in the Hellenic.

"We are, of course, grateful for your information about the stranded spatiotemporal vehicle. It can be repaired and returned. Yes, you can yourselves be sent back. Precisely because the control fields failed and thus caused the original trouble, we have (figuratively speaking) an energy lane where the machine passed through the continuum. Launched back along that, the vehicle can carry you, can leave you off where and when you were first picked up, in an exact reversal of the original accidental process.

"Repairs will take a while, given our scanty facilities. Furthermore, you have been through terrible experiences. We are based at the Black Sea, well away from the stricken area. Would you not like to be flown there, to rest, recover, and decide just what you want to make of the lives you have gained?"

Oleg had said, sentimentally and rather drunkenly: "Last night together, eh? I won't spoil it for you two, any more than I've been bothering you much these past weeks. I'll miss you, though, however glad to come home." He gave them each a bear hug and wandered off to bed.

Reid and Erissa were alone. The futurian expedition housed itself not in a tent but in a building whose arches soared airy, iridescent, and indestructible as rainbows. From the terrace where they stood, a hillside dropped in forest that was sweet with summer, hoar with moonlight, to broad and quiet waters. Overhead were many stars. A nightingale sang.

"I almost wish we could stay," he said in awkwardness.

She shook her head. "We've talked this out, darling. Exile would not be well for either of us. Worse would be knowing how much love we betrayed in our homes."

"It seems so hollow," he said in the pain of tomorrow's loss. "We did nothing but come full circle, except that you learned the core of your life was a lie."

"Oh, but we did far more!" she exclaimed. Laying hands on his shoulders, she regarded him gravely and tenderly. "Haven't you understood? Must I tell you anew? We lived that half year, and if we met grief, we also found joy in each other which will dwell with us till we die. And we have our victory—for it was a victory, that we and those in our care outlived the end of a world and even saved much of it for the world which is to follow. If we had only a single road to walk, that twisted back on itself, still, we walked it. I see now that we never were slaves to fate, because our own wills were what made that destiny for us.

"I gave myself a myth. But the young and wounded need myths. Lately I have outgrown the need, and truth is better. Oh, it hurt for a while, Duncan, hurt bitterly. I have you to thank for showing me that Deukalion is truly my beloved oldest son, that his life is a pledge of an end to hatred. And my man Dagonas, why, I'll never lie in his arms again without remembering the sight of how he watched over that girl. You are no longer my god, you are my dear friend, which is more; and he is my life's man."

She paused; then, slowly: "No, there is no pure happiness. But I am going to be happier than I was. I hope you likewise will be, Duncan."

He kissed her. "I believe that," he said. "You healed me of a lameness I didn't know I had."

She smiled. "Tonight is ours. But my dear whom soon I must bid goodbye, first tell me once more of what is to come."

"A thousand years hence, Athens shines in a glory that will gladden the rest of mankind's time on earth. And its secret seed is that heritage it got from your people."

"There is comfort to live by: that my country was, that theirs will be. Now let us be only us two."

He stumbled, fell, and lay a minute on the pulsing deck while the dizziness of his flight passed away.

But I'd better rise, he thought, and get into our cabin before somebody comes by. In spite of the shave and haircut and imitation of twentieth-century clothes they gave me, I'll have trouble explaining some changes in my appearance.

He lifted himself erect. Strength returned, and calm. The North Pacific shimmered and murmured around him. He tried to summon Erissa's image out of the moonlight, but already that was hard to do, as if he sought to recall a dream.

And yet, he realized, she helped me win everything. She

taught me what it is to be a woman, and so what it is to be a man.

He went below. Pamela lay propped in her bunk, alone with a softcover mystery novel. The lamplight glowed on her hair and on the picture of their children. She glanced up. "Oh," she said timidly. "You're back sooner than I expected."

He smiled at her. It came to him that earlier this night he had been recalling a man who died young of senseless causes, but who first lived more than most. Among the words he left:

> —*And so I never feared to see*
>    *You wander down the street,*
> *Or come across the fields to me*
>    *On ordinary feet.*
> *For what they'd never told me of,*
>    *And what I never knew,*
> *It was that all the time, my love,*
>    *Love would be merely you.*

Pamela looked closer at Reid and sat straight. "Why, you've a different coat on," she said. "And—"

"Well, you see, a crewman and I got talking, decided we liked each other's coats better, and swapped," he replied. "Here, inspect." He slipped the garment off and tossed it onto her lap. She couldn't help staring at it, feeling the unfamiliar material. Meanwhile he scrambled out of the rest and, under cover of donning a bathrobe, dropped the pieces in a drawer. He'd toss them overboard later.

She raised her eyes again. "Duncan," she said. "You're suddenly thin. And those creases in your face—"

"Do you mean you hadn't noticed?" He lowered himself to the side of her bunk, cupped her chin in his hand, and said: "It's past time we stopped drifting apart. Break out your oars, mate, and if you're not sure how to use them, let me show you."

I must distract her, he thought. Someday I'll tell her the whole truth. But not yet. She couldn't believe. Anyhow, we've more important business first.

I feel the new thing in me, the knowing what is needed, the spirit that does not surrender, the courage to be joyful.

"What do you mean?" she pleaded.

He answered: "I want to make my woman happy."